D1627391

# I AM SLAUGHTER

THE BEAST ARISES

BOOK ONE

# I AM SLAUGHTER

DAN ABNETT

BLACK LIBRARY

*With thanks to Nick and Nik*

**A BLACK LIBRARY PUBLICATION**

First published in Great Britain in 2015 by
Black Library
Games Workshop Ltd
Willow Road
Nottingham NG7 2WS UK

10 9 8 7 6 5 4 3 2 1

Produced by Games Workshop in Nottingham

A CIP record for this book is available from the British Library.

UK ISBN 13: 978 1 78496 054 4
US ISBN 13: 978 1 78496 067 4

See Black Library on the internet at
# blacklibrary.com

Find out more about Games Workshop
and the world of Warhammer 40,000 at
# games-workshop.com

Printed and bound in China

*Fire sputters...*
*The shame of our deaths*
*and our heresies is done. They are*
*behind us, like wretched phantoms. This*
*is a new age, a strong age, an age of Imperium.*
*Despite our losses, despite the fallen sons, despite the*
*eternal silence of the Emperor, now watching over us in*
*spirit instead of in person, we will endure. There will be no*
*more war on such a perilous scale. There will be an end*
*to wanton destruction. Yes, foes will come and*
*enemies will arise. Our security will be*
*threatened, but we will be ready, our*
*mighty fists raised. There will be no*
*great war to challenge us now.*
*We will not be brought*
*to the brink like that*
*again...*

# ONE

The Chromes were relatively easy to kill, but they came in ferocious numbers.

Eight walls of Imperial Fists boxed one of their primary family groups into a scrub-sided valley east of the blister-nest, and reduced them to burned shells and spattered meat.

Smoke rose off the hill of dead. It was a yellowish air-stain composed of atomised organic particulates and the back-wash of fyceline smoke. According to the magos biologis sent to assist the undertaking, sustained bolter and las-fire, together with the chronic impact trauma of blade and close-combat weapons, had effectively aerosolised about seven per cent of the enemy's collective biomass. The yel-low smoke, a cloud twenty kilometres wide and sixty long, drained down the valley like a dawn fog.

The magos biologis told Koorland this as if the fact had some practical application. Koorland, second captain of Daylight Wall Company, shrugged. It was a non-fact to him, like someone saying the shape of a pool of spilled blood

resembled a map of Arcturus or Great-Uncle Janier's profile. Koorland had been sent to Throne-forsaken Ardamantua to kill Chromes. He was used to killing things. He was good at it, like all his company brothers and like every brother of the shield-corps. He was also used to the fact that when things were killed in colossal numbers, it left a mess. Sometimes the mess was smoke, sometimes it was liquid, sometimes it was grease, sometimes it was embers. He didn't need some Terra-spire expert telling him that he and his brothers had pounded the Chromes so hard and so explosively that they had vaporised part of them.

The magos biologis had a retinue of three hundred acolytes and servitors. They were hooded and diligent, and had decorated the hillside with portable detection equipment and analysis engines. Tubes sniffed the air (this, Koorland understood, was how the magos biologis had arrived at his seven per cent revelation). Picting and imaging devices recorded the anatomies of dead and living Chrome specimens alike. Dissections were underway.

'The Chromes are not a high-factor hostile species,' the magos told Koorland.

'Really?' Koorland replied through his visor speakers, obliged to listen to the report.

'Not at all,' the human said, shaking his head, apparently under the impression that Koorland's obligation was in fact interest. 'See for yourself,' he said, gesturing to a half-flayed specimen spread-eagled on a dissection stand. 'They are armoured, of course, around the head, neck and back, and their forelimbs are well formed into digital blades–'

'Or "claws",' said Koorland.

'Just so,' the magos went on, 'especially in sub-adult and adult males. They are not harmless, but they are not a naturally aggressive species.'

Koorland thought about that. The Chromes – so called because of the silvery metallic finish of their chitin armour – were xenosbreed, human-sized bugs with long forelimbs and impressive speed. He thought about the eighteen million of them that had swarmed the valley that afternoon, the sea of silver gleaming in the sunlight, the swish of their bladed limbs, the *tek-tek-tek* noise they made with their mouthparts, like broken cogitators. He thought of the three brothers he'd lost from his wall during the initial overwhelm, the four taken from Hemispheric Wall, the three from Anterior Six Gate Wall.

Go tell them *not naturally aggressive.*

The Chromes had numbers, vast numbers. The more they had killed, the more there were to kill. Sustained slaughter was the only operational tactic: keep killing them until they were all dead. The rate at which the Imperial Fists had been required to hit them, the duration, the frenzy – no damn wonder they aerosolised seven per cent of their biomass.

'Chromes have been encountered on sixty-six other worlds in this sector alone,' said the magos biologis. 'Twenty-four of those encounters took place during compliance expeditions at the time of the Great Crusade, the rest since. Chromes have been encountered in large numbers, and have often defended themselves. They have never been known to behave with such proactive hostility before.'

The magos thought about this.

'They remind me of rats,' he said. 'Rad-rats. I remember

there was a terrible plague of them down in the basements and sub-basements under the archive block of the Biologis Sanctum at Numis. They were destroying valuable specimens and records, but they were not, individually, in any way harmful or dangerous. We sent in environmental purge teams with flame guns and toxin sprays. We began to exterminate them. They swarmed. Fear, I suppose. They came flooding out of the place and we lost three men and a dozen servitors in the deluge. Unstoppable. Like the sub-hive rats, the Chromes have never behaved this way before.'

'And they won't again,' said Koorland, 'because when we're finished here they'll all be dead.'

'This is just one of a possible nineteen primary family groups,' said the magos biologis. He paused. Koorland knew that the magos intended to address him by name, but, like so many humans, he found it difficult to differentiate between the giant, transhuman warriors in their yellow armour. He had to rely on rank pins, insignia and the unit markings on shoulderplates, and that information always took a moment to process.

The magos biologis nodded slightly, as if to apologise for the hesitation.

'–Captain Koorland of the Second Daylight Wall–'

'I'm second captain of the Daylight Wall Company,' Koorland corrected.

'Ah, of course.'

'Forget about rank, just try to remember us by our wall-names.'

'Your what?'

Koorland sighed. This man knew more than seemed

healthy about xenosbreeds, but he knew nothing about the warriors built to guard against them.

'Our wall-names,' he said. 'When we are inducted, we forget our given names, our pre-breed names. Our brothers bestow upon each of us a name that suits our bearing or character: a wall-name.'

The magos nodded, politely interested.

Koorland gestured to a Space Marine trudging past them.

'That's Firefight,' he said. 'That brother over there? He's Dolorous. Him there? Killshot.'

'I see,' said the magos biologis. 'These are earned names, names within the brotherhood.'

Koorland nodded. He knew that, at some point, he'd been told the magos biologis' name. He hadn't forgotten because it was complicated, he just hadn't cared enough about the human to remember it.

'What is your name, captain?' the magos asked brightly. 'Your wall-name?'

'My name?' Koorland replied. 'I am Slaughter.'

# TWO

## Ardamantua

In less than six solar hours, they were back in combat.

A filthy dusk had settled over the landscape. In the reddish haze of the sky, the low-anchored bulks of their barges hung like oblong, tusk-prowed moons. The Chapter Master had ordered over ninety per cent of the Fists' strength out on this undertaking. It was a huge show of force. Too much, in Slaughter's opinion. But it was political too. The Adeptus Astartes were very good at prosecuting and finishing wars. Whenever extended periods of peace broke out, especially in the exalted systems and holdings around the Terran Core, it became harder to justify the sheer might of a standing army like the Imperial Fists. It was good to get them out, to give them purpose, to chalk up a staggering victory that the core system populations could celebrate. The extermination of a xenosbreed threat like the Chromes was ample justification for such lethal institutions as the Imperial Fists.

Strategic surveys put the Chrome numbers at something in the order of eighty-eight billion, and migratory scans showed a pronounced in-curve diaspora towards the core worlds. Besides, Ardamantua, Throne-forsaken Ardamantua, was just six warp-weeks from Solar Approach.

Since the very earliest ages of the Imperium, the Imperial Fists had been the primary defenders of Terra. Other Chapters – Legions, as they had been known, until the Great Heresy and the instigation of the Codex – might crusade, explore or take war to the furthest corners of Imperial space. But the Imperial Fists were the primary guardians of Terra and the core. This was what they had always done. This was the duty their beloved Primarch-Progenitor had charged them with when he had left them.

It was their legacy.

Surface scans had shown another Chrome family group of significant size moving around the blisternest. Daylight Wall had led the way across the river, with two walls at their heels and another crossing further up. The river was broad but slow and heavy, no more than waist-deep, and muddy. The brackish water fumed with insects.

The Chromes started to resist when they saw the Imperial Fists wading out to the nest side. Some plunged into the water and attempted to attack. Shooting began, brothers firing from the soupy water, pushing the foe back, driving the Chromes up the claggy banks even as the xenos gathered in greater numbers to plunge in. The enemy became agitated. The slow tide was soon full of Chrome corpses, spinning end to end as they drifted downstream. The Imperial Fists advance seemed almost sullen; they came slowly, trudging through the stinking water, firing because they had to at targets too ridiculously easy to hit.

Slaughter roused his men. If they were going to engage, they were going to do it with dignity. They were coming up the bank, approaching the huge, septic shape of the blisternest rim.

'Daylight Wall stands forever,' he voxed. 'No wall stands against it. Bring them down.'

The men of the company clashed their boltguns and their broadswords against their combat shields and chanted the refrain back. The advance began to accelerate.

A wall of men. A wall of supermen.

Slaughter reached the bank. It was a steep, slick mire threaded with coarse vegetation. Glinting in the smoky light, Chromes bounded down onto the ridges, rising up into threat postures and challenging him. He came out of the water, oily green moisture trailing off his yellow armour. Frenzy was at his left hand, Heartshot was at his right.

The first of the Chromes came at him.

Slaughter's broadsword was a two-handed power blade with a silver cross-hilt and a black pommel. It had fought at Terra, during the Siege, in the hands of a Fist called Emetris, who had fallen there. It was as broad as a standard human male's thigh. He brought it up and it described an arc in the air as the first Chrome leapt. It split the xenos through its gleaming bio-armour and cut it in two. Ichor showered in all directions. A second sprang, and he smashed it aside, slashed open. A third met the blade, impaled itself, and thrashed wildly until he ripped the sword back out.

It was just the beginning. They started to rush. A dozen, two dozen, all at once. Slaughter liked sword-work. It was economical. It saved munitions for more significant moments.

The broadsword was a finely balanced instrument in his huge hands. The two-handed grip could turn and shear each swing in a surprisingly subtle number of ways.

Slaughter began to slaughter.

He left a trail of dead behind him: ruptured silver husks weeping ichor into the matted, trampled vegetation. Each step was an impact as another two or three Chromes came at him and were met by the brute, full-stop force of his blade. Organic debris flew from each killstroke. Ichor and other xenos fluids squirted high into the air and dappled his armour like dew, like rain.

Frenzy tore through the stand of dry weeds to his left, swinging an axe that had been the proud possession of a series of Fists since before the Great Crusade. The curve of its bite had been notched by the skull of a green warboss during the Malla Vajjl compliance. Frenzy, a big-hearted generous man, possessed particularly acute hand-eye coordination. His movements were so fast and precise, they seemed almost random. He had earned his wall-name through his grace on the field, the constant motion, the changing grips, the reversals, the back-steps, the aggression. His axe moved from grip to grip like a baton or a staff whirled by some ceremonial parade-ground officer. It seemed to fly from his hand many times as he turned and changed position, but it never left him. Like Slaughter, he had eschewed his bolter for the clearance work.

Slaughter wished he could stop and admire the battle-craft of his friend and brother, but there was no opportunity. The enemy's numbers were increasing.

To Slaughter's right, tearing through the reed beds and the

dried mucus walls of the blisternest edges, came Heartshot and Chokehold. Heartshot's rotary cannon made a metallic din like a stamp-press forge at full production. Chokehold's bolter exploded two or sometimes three charging Chromes with each shcll.

Slaughter barked orders, kept the line firm. He didn't want over-step. He didn't want the Chromes to find a way in through any gap in their line. Heartshot and Chokehold moved ahead fast, cutting their path with firepower. He had to keep them leashed.

He called out wall-names – Cleaver, Arm's Length, Cold-eye, Lifetaker, Bleedout – and urged them in at the back, ordering them through the reed beds to fill and cover.

His head snapped around from a sideways blow. He smelled blood in his nose, blood that clotted instantly. A screamer alert sang in his helm and his visor display blinked up mottled damage patterns.

He recovered. This took less than a second. One of the big adults had raked his head with a forelimb claw. He'd taken his eye off the fight for a micro-moment to check the line.

His sword killed the thing for its insult and for the scratch it left in the yellow surface of his helm. But there was another at its heels, an even bigger adult. It was two-thirds his size. He hadn't seen Chromes this big before. Its appearance was different too. It was not chrome or silvery. Its chitin and armour, and its claws, seemed resiny black and brown, as if made from a horny bark that was still growing.

It ripped his chestplate. Slaughter got his shield in the way, took off its limb mid-forearm, and then reversed his blade and killed it.

Two strokes for one kill. Inefficient.

The thing had been big. It had required the extra effort.

Another large, dark form appeared, and then two more. What were they? A sub-species? A larger, more aggressive form of the basic Chrome xenotype?

Slaughter's helm was alive with vox-chatter reports from across the offensive, all describing the same new type: larger, darker, bigger, stronger, harder to kill.

Tactical re-evaluation. Slaughter started to issue advisories even as he met the next of the new kind. Two strokes to kill one, three to finish the next. More gouges down to bare metal on his armour.

Why would any force, any species, keep its largest and strongest warrior-forms in reserve? Why would they not send them out into open combat? They might have halted or driven back the Adeptus Astartes' attack long before they had cut their way to the blisternest.

The *tek-tek-tek* noise the Chromes made with their mouth-parts, that malfunctioning data-engine clatter, was changing. The bigger, darker warrior-forms made a lower, duller noise, a *clack-clack-clack*. Two brothers in the line had already fallen to their superior power and savagery.

'Do we fall back?' Frenzy voxed. 'Slaughter, do we break and regroup? This is new. This is–'

'Hold the line,' Slaughter replied. 'No regroup. No fall back. Hold the line. Daylight Wall stands forever. No wall stands against it. Bring them down.'

'Understood.'

Frenzy's unquestioning *understood* was instantly echoed by a hundred voxed voices.

Slaughter ducked a slashing brown claw the size of Frenzy's axe-head. He was smiling.

He had made a realisation. He knew what this was.

*They are us. They are Daylight Wall.*

The blisternest was the Chromes' Palace of Terra. They had kept their bravest and best and mightiest warriors in reserve to defend it, in case an enemy ever got through.

This was their last ditch. Their last stand. This was their final wall, their do or die.

The Imperial Fists were just hours away from completing their undertaking to Ardamantua and adding another proud tally to their glory roll.

This was the bloody endgame, and it would be a battle to relish.

'Hold the line,' Slaughter ordered. Then, as a practical afterthought, he added, 'Use your bolters.'

# THREE

## Terra – the Imperial Palace

The air was smoke.

In preparation for the midday Senatorum meeting, servitors had lit the burners in the upper galleries and the approach halls, and in the alcoves along the Walk of Heroes, whose great leaded windows, miraculously spared by the pounding overpressure of the Siege, had looked out onto the stately yards behind Eternity Gate for two dozen centuries.

The burners fumed with camphor and septrewood, rose-ash and parvum, the sacred incense of the Saviour Emperor, thought to smell exactly like the incorruptible sanctity of His Eternal Form.

Vangorich couldn't attest to this. Given his office as a Grand Master, he might have requested, and even been granted, the chance to show observance at the foot of the Golden Throne. He had never bothered. The dead did not interest him, not even the divine dead. What interested him – obsessed him – were the mechanisms by which things

*became* dead, and the opportunities those deaths afforded the living.

He had entered the Inner Palace that morning through West Watch, and then followed the hallway walks behind the High Gardens and Daylight Wall before pausing in the chapel ordinary behind the cloister wall to make a small devotion at the basin font.

Vangorich was not a pious man. He was a man of faith, but it was not a spiritual faith. He made his devotion because he knew – or at least could be fairly certain – that agents from a dozen or more ministries and factions were watching him at all hours of the day and night. It was easier to make sure he was seen to be doing what he was supposed to do, than it was to waste manpower eradicating those spies on a daily basis.

Let his rivals do the hard work. It was no great effort to act a part.

Drakan Vangorich had been doing it all his life.

So he did what was expected of him. As a Grand Master – albeit of an Officio that had once been powerful and was now regarded as an atavistic throwback to a more brutal age – he was expected to attend all meetings, formal and discretionary. He was supposed to show humility and dignity. He was supposed not to express any cruel or bloodthirsty appetites, the sort of appetites his rivals assumed that a Grand Master of the Officio Assassinorum must harbour. He was supposed to show respect to the Creed.

All Senatorum members took a blessing or expressed some devotion before taking their seats at meetings, so that the will of the God-Emperor might guide their thoughts

and wisdom. Some, like the odious Lansung, made a great
show of doing so, in full dress uniform, usually in the
chapel-vault of one of his battlefleet vessels in orbit. Mesring was the same, leading a train of gowned, gold-helmed
savant-priests into the rotunda church below Hemispheric
Wall. Pompous idiots!

Vangorich, dressed in simple, ascetic black, opted for a
less showy effect. The chapel ordinary was used by Palace servants and householders for their daily observances.
It was not a public place, just a very plain cell with frugal
appointments. Vangorich was aware that using it made him
look dutiful, restrained, and very humble. It made him look
more admirably spiritual than the lords who made their
observances for show. It spoke of simplicity and a lack of
arrogance.

It made him look trustworthy and noble. It made him
look good. He liked his rivals' spies to see that. He knew it
irked them beyond measure to hear that he had stopped for
a few minutes in a private, unostentatious servants' chapel
to make a discreet act of faith. How it bothered them that
he was so unimpeachably wholesome.

The truth was, he probably thought more about how he
looked at all times, and what his image said about him, than
the likes of Mesring and Lansung. Their activities were conducted publicly, to win popular support; Vangorich's were
conducted simply for the benefit of the ever-circling spies.
He performed for his rivals, playing the part he wanted
them to see.

How would they see him now, coming to the meeting?
As a man of medium height and medium build, dressed in

black, with black hair oiled back like a clerk's across his narrow skull. His skin was pale from the constant twilight of life in the Palace, and he had precious little in the way of distinguishing features, except for his dark, wide-set eyes and the duelling scar that canyoned the left part of his mouth and chin.

Vangorich never spoke of the duel, except to say that it had happened when he was a youth, before he took office, and he regretted it in as much as the matter should not have been resolved face-to-face with rapiers, but rather with him placed behind his adversary, dagger in hand, and his adversary unaware of his presence.

Drakan Vangorich liked to kill things. He liked to kill things as efficiently as possible, with the least possible effort, and he only ever killed things if there was a reason: a good reason, a persuasive reason. Death was the pure solution to life's greatest and most confounding problems.

This was what so many of the offices and agencies seemed not to understand about the ancient Officio Assassinorum. It was not an archaic killing machine, lurking to spread disorder and mayhem at the whim of some mercurial Grand Master, poisoning here and stabbing there. It was not a thirsty sword hung in a rack, aching to shed blood.

It was a necessary and purifying fire. It was the last resort, the end of arguments. It was hope and it was salvation. It was the noblest and truest of all the Offices of Terra.

The Emperor had understood this, which was why He had instigated the office and allowed it to function during His lifetime. He had understood the necessity for ultimate sanction. He had, after all, permitted the VI Legion of the

Adeptus Astartes to exist simply to function in that role as it applied to primarchs and other Legions. Grand Master Vangorich's office existed to perform that function at a court level.

That was why the other lords were afraid of him. They all presumed he might stab them in the spine. They always forgot that he was their instrument. *They* got to vote on who he killed. *They* should spend more time worrying about each other.

'Good day, Daylight,' he said as he stepped out of the chapel ordinary to continue his walk to the Great Chamber.

The Imperial Fist, his armour polished and perfect, turned slowly and offered Vangorich a shallow tip of the head.

'Good day, Grand Master,' the Space Marine replied, his voice welling up as a volcanic rumble through helm-speakers. He towered over the human lord, ornamental spear in his left fist, litany-inscribed shield in his right. Vangorich felt sorry for the wall-brothers of the VII. They were reputed to be the very finest of all, the most excellent and capable of their Chapter. Yet, because of ritual and ceremony and honour, they were fated to remain here for their entire service lives; the best of the best, one for each of the Palace walls that the Fists had protected, wasting their immense potential, serving out their time in the one place in the galaxy that war would never visit again.

They didn't even have names. They simply wore the names of the walls they patrolled, every day and night, in perfectly polished armour.

'I'm probably late for the meeting,' Vangorich remarked.

'You have six minutes and thirteen seconds remaining,

sir,' replied the Space Marine. 'However, I suggest you take Gilded Walk to the traverse behind Anterior Six Gate.'

'Because they're not meeting in the Great Chamber?'

The Space Marine nodded.

'They are not, sir.'

'They keep doing that,' said Vangorich, peeved. 'I think it is unseemly. The Great Chamber was good enough for our ancestors. It was built as our parliament.'

'Times change, sir,' said the warrior Daylight.

Vangorich paused and looked up at the grim and unfathomable visor. Light glowed like coals behind the optic lenses.

'Do they?' he asked. 'Do you wish for that, Daylight? Do you wish for the chance to kill?'

'With every fibre of my soul, and every second of my life, sir,' the Imperial Fist replied. 'But this is the duty I have been given and I will perform it with my entire heart and will.'

Vangorich felt he ought to say something, but he could not think of anything adequate, so he nodded, turned, and walked away down the gloomy hallway.

# FOUR

## Terra – the Imperial Palace

The Great Chamber had been the seat of power on Terra since the Palace had been established. It was a formidable stadium, a veritable colosseum, with a central dais and seats for the High Lords, and then vast tiers of seats for the more minor officials and lords, lesser functionaries, petitioners and so forth. At full capacity, it could hold half a million people. It had been damaged during the Siege, but it had been restored and repaired in a sympathetic fashion. A huge statue of Rogal Dorn had been erected at the east end, commemorating his superhuman efforts of defence in general, and his extraordinary running battle in the hallways just outside that very place.

It had not been Dorn's choice. Guilliman had ordered the statue raised.

'My brother watched over the Palace during our darkest hour,' he had said. 'He should watch over the council evermore.'

Of late, in the last few decades, the Senatorum Imperialis had taken to meeting in other places. The Great Chamber was too big for anything except full meetings, many claimed: too noisy, too formal. Favour was placed on more closed sessions, in smaller chambers, for intimacy and immediacy. The Clanium Library was often used, almost as a private cabinet. Sometimes, the High Lords convened in the Anesidoran Chapel.

Most preferred was the Cerebrium, a comparatively small, wood-panelled room near the top of the Widdershins Tower. It was said that the Emperor had favoured the rooms of the tower for meditation and mindfulness, and the Cerebrium in particular. 'It makes us feel closer to His thoughts to convene here,' Udo had once exclaimed, defending the regular use of the room.

Vangorich knew perfectly well why they did it.

The Cerebrium had a large, figured wooden table at its centre, and the table was big enough to take twelve chairs.

Only the twelve members of the High Senatorum could sit in session together. Secondary officials, like Vangorich, were obliged to lurk in the shadows, or take seats along the wall.

It was power play. It was infantile.

The Cerebrium was a fine room, well-appointed and quite atmospheric. Opening the casement shutters afforded the room an extraordinary view across the Palace roofscape and down over the ring-gates and the armoured flanks of the world. Vangorich had often thought it would make an excellent private study or office.

However, it was hardly a place to run the Imperium from. It was too small, too insubstantial, too amateurish. It was a back-room, fit only for private thoughts and back-room deals. It was not a place of government.

Vangorich entered, his attendance solemnly noted by the servitor of record. The High Lords were taking their seats. He nodded a greeting with Lord Militant Heth, his only true ally among the High Twelve, and then found a place in the flip-down wooden pews under the east windows, where other lesser lords and functionaries were seating themselves. They greeted him as if he was one of them.

He was not.

Less than a century before, one of the permanent seats among the High Twelve had belonged to the Grand Master of the Officio Assassinorum. The office was one of the 'Old Twelve' that had sat in governance of the Imperium since the Senatorum's inception.

Times, as Brother Daylight had said, were changing. Some offices, and none more than the Office of Assassins, were now seen as obsolete at best, or archaic and primitive at worst. They had been edged out of the inner twelve, and either dispensed with altogether, or relegated to the lesser seats outside the High Circle. Other, newer, stations had advanced in their place.

This was ignominious. Vangorich accepted that some of the Imperium's newer institutions absolutely deserved a seat at the table. Both the agents of the Inquisition and the ecclesiarchs of the Ministorum required representation among the High Lords since the Heresy War. They were fundamental parts of the modern Imperium. Vangorich would not argue that. What he would argue was that the council should have been expanded to admit them rather than culled to find them places.

He watched them take their seats at the table, talking

together, some laughing. Wienand, the Inquisitorial Representative, was the only one not talking to anybody. She was quiet and reserved and surprisingly young, with sharp cheekbones and very short, steel-grey hair. Technically, she was his replacement. Technically, the Inquisitorial Representative had taken the permanent seat that had traditionally belonged to the Grand Master of the Officio Assassinorum.

Vangorich held no grudge. He quite liked Wienand, and he'd admired her predecessor. He believed in the near-autonomous function of the Inquisition, because it reflected, in spirit, the same safety-catch mechanism as the Assassinorum. He often met with Wienand and others of her kind, in private of course, to discuss operational techniques, methodology of detection and research, jurisdiction, and also to share inter-agency intelligence. He found that the inquisitors were often astonished at the level of intelligence his office was able to gather, and they often turned to him, clandestinely, for favours.

It was all part of the give and take.

Heth was the Lord Commander Militant of the Astra Militarum, an old, maimed veteran. Though the Guard was the largest military body in the Imperium, Heth felt it to be very much the junior third service to the Adeptus Astartes and the Navy. It was probably why he sought out unlikely allies with voting rights, such as Vangorich.

Lansung was certainly ignoring him. Lansung, broad, red of face and booming of voice, was the Lord High Admiral of the Imperial Navy. His corpulent form was encased in a uniform of oceanic blue threaded with silver braid. He took a while to be seated, engaging Tobris Ekharth, the Master of the Administratum, in some convoluted piece of scandal-mongering while Vernor Zeck looked on with patient indulgence. Zeck, the giant among them, was the Grand Provost Marshal of the Adeptus Arbitrators. He was one of the two most heavily augmented humans among the High Twelve. He was not particularly amused or even diverted by Lansung's outrageous gossip, but he was forcing himself to at least feign a show of interest. Vangorich was aware that Zeck's mind was a billion light years away, processing the layers of administrative and forensic data, the ceaseless work of keeping Terra's gargantuan hives ordered and policed. The look of wry amusement on his leonine face was a simulation for Lansung's benefit.

Similarly, Lansung wasn't at all interested in speaking to Ekharth, other than to cultivate the loyalties between Navy and Administratum. He was telling a story at Ekharth so he could get Zeck's attention, and be seen to be the close and genuine confidant of the Provost Marshal.

Maybe I should draw up a map, thought Vangorich. A map or chart, some kind of visual aid, a diagram of the basic interpersonal relations of the High Twelve. It could be colour-coded to reveal areas of contempt, deceit, insincerity, political expediency and outright rancour. Yes, I might do that and present it to the Senatorum one day under 'any other business', he thought.

At the other end of the table, Kubik, the Fabricator General of the Adeptus Mechanicus, was conducting a dialogue with Mesring, the Ecclesiarch of the Adeptus Ministorum, and Helad Gibran, the Paternoval Envoy of the Navigators.

Kubik was, of course, the other extensively augmented person present, but his alterations had been elective and had begun at an early age, rather than being the result of repair and injury like Zeck's. Vangorich watched Kubik's actions and movements with great interest. He had only limited experience of killing servants of the Mechanicus, and it was a skill he felt he ought to develop given the vast political and materiel power of Mars. He thought, instinctively, they would be hard to kill. The Navigators, equally inhuman, at least seemed physically frail and vulnerable.

Vangorich had already prepared methodologies on some of the other 'sub-species' at the table. The haunted, spectral servants of the Astronomican, represented in the High Twelve by Volquan Sark, the Master of the Astronomican, were still human enough for conventional processes. The telepaths... Ah, the telepaths were a different order of things. Abdulias Anwar, the Master of the Adeptus Astra Telepathica, was typical of their malevolent and discomforting kind. To deal with telepaths, with the Imperium's most powerful sanctioned telepaths... Well, that was why Vangorich had brokered such close ties with Wienand and her ilk.

Juskina Tull, the Speaker for the Chartist Captains, was the eleventh of the High Twelve. A magnificent woman in an almost theatrically ostentatious gown, she occupied a role that many thought was the most trivial of all the seats. On the other hand, the Merchant Fleets represented nearly ninety per cent of the Imperium's interstellar capability. In times of crisis, the Speaker wielded power greater than the Lord High Admiral.

A bell sounded. The delegates moved to their places, even

the most exalted of them. Cherub servitors and vox-recorder drones buzzed around the Cerebrium as though it were an aviary.

Lord Guilliman entered the crowded, panelled chamber and took his seat. He bowed his head to his eleven senior fellows. He was the Lord Commander of the Imperium, the commander-in-chief of all Imperial military assets. His head was shaved, and the huge old scar traversing his scalp and neck was very visible. Though beyond any single discipline or arm of the Imperial war machine, he wore a braided uniform that was, in style at least, an echo of the grand admiral's uniform he had worn during his illustrious pre-Senatorum career.

His name was Udin Macht Udo. He was not the first human to hold the chair of the Senatorum Imperialis, but like all his predecessors, human and transhuman alike, he used the formal, honorary title of his office, the name of the first Lord Commander: Guilliman of Macragge.

Udo glanced around the chamber. His eyes, the left one glazed and milky under the lip of the long scar, fixed upon Ekharth, the Master of the Administratum.

'Bring us to order, sir,' Lord Guilliman said.

Ekharth nodded, activated the cogitator-recorder that was crouching on the table in front of him, and began to type on the quivering spindle keys that unfurled from it like the wings of a giant moth.

'High Lords, we are now in session,' Ekharth began.

# FIVE

## Ardamantua

The loops and coils of the tunnels ahead resonated with the dull *clack-clack-clack* noise that told Slaughter what was waiting for them.

More fierce resistance. More of the new, more powerful warrior-forms. Many more.

The Imperial Fists had smashed and torn their way into the outer layers of the Chromes' huge blisternest. Daylight Wall had made the first entry, an honour mark for their company, and then Hemispheric Wall had punched through about ten minutes later on the far side of the vast edifice's sloping sides. Brothers of the shield-corps were now pouring into the alien nightmare of the Chromes' nest through two dozen breaches.

The blisternest was an organic structure the size of a large Terran hive. Its walls, compartments, chambers and linking tunnels were curved and organic, and seemed to have been formed or grown from some greyish, semi-transparent material that had been extruded and then woven, hardening in the air. From the outside, it looked like a swollen blister. Inside, it was like venturing through the chambers of some alien heart. There was a general dampness and humidity, and sections of the structure throbbed and pulsed wetly, heaving with pus-like fluids that pumped and writhed through the building's skin. The compartments and chambers inside were more like valves and organic voids, the spaces inside living structures. There was mould and fungal growth, and pockets of vapour. The echoing tubes throbbed with the *tek-tek-tek* sound, and the deeper agitation of the more powerful warrior-forms.

At regular intervals the interior sounds generated by the nation of Chromes were drowned out as airstrike support howled in overhead. Low-flying attack runs left blossoming trails of firestorm fury in their wake, engulfing the upper levels of the blisternest. Flights of Caestus rams, specialist vehicles designed for ship-boarding actions, had been unleashed too, driving their armoured prows into the skin of the vast nest to deliver assault squads of shield-corps brothers.

Slaughter waged his own war through the dank, miasmal chambers. The muzzle-flash of his bolter, jumping and sun-bright, lit up the green twilight of the nest. He kept his sword drawn. The big warrior-forms tended to get the bolter rounds. The regular Chromes met his blade's edge. In places, the dipping, curved floor of the nest tunnels was ankle-deep in swilling Chrome ichor. The standing fluid reflected the crackling light of multiple fires, and crimped with ripple patterns every time an airstrike shook the ground.

A pack of Chromes rushed him down the flue of a tunnel.

Slaughter stood his ground and set in with sword and bolt-gun. Severed or exploded aliens peeled away on either side of his resolute form, or were hurled backwards into their kin. Slaughter bellowed the battle cry of Daylight Wall, and urged his brothers up the ducts and grimy arterial conduits that the nest used as corridors.

His yellow armour was flecked with soot and slime. He smashed a charging Chrome away from him with the back of his fist. The thing broke as it hit the nest wall and left a spatter of juice as it slid down. One of the bigger, darker things attacked. With a grim smile, Slaughter realised he was thinking of these things as 'veterans'. They were the old guard. He admired their skill and their power. They had fought wars for their benighted race out among the stars. He could see that in them. They had protected their own and perhaps conquered territory. He wondered which xenos species they had battled that he had also fought.

The first thing a good warrior always did was respect his enemy. He evaluated and assessed his foe, and woe betide him if he failed to appreciate what his opponent brought to the field. Slaughter had nothing but appropriate respect for the 'veterans'. He'd seen them gut and dice enough of his shield-brothers that day already. The losses were going to be high. At least, he reflected, the damn lordlings and politicos would be pleased. The war against the Chrome advance was proving that serious threats still remained, and that military forces like the Imperial Fists were not expensive luxuries.

The second captain met the veteran's approach with his blade, deflecting the scything claws of the upper limbs. The veteran was strong, and managed to smash the sword out of Slaughter's grip.

He cursed and shot it through the brain case with his bolter. The entire front of his armour was sprayed an instant grey. Another lumbered towards him and he shot that too, blowing out its midsection and snapping its spinal membranes. Frenzy finished the next with his axe.

'Getting tired, captain?' Heartshot asked Slaughter.

Slaughter told him what he could do with his rotor cannon, and then retrieved his sword.

'Anterior Six and Ballad Gateway are now in the nest with us,' reported Frenzy, his voice a vox-buzz.

'That's good enough,' said Slaughter. 'Four walls should bring this place down.'

'There are assault squads from Zarathustra in the upper levels too,' said Coldeye.

'We can close the book,' said Slaughter. 'By the next time the wretched local star rises, we–'

His words were drowned out. A sudden and deep noise boiled out of the guts of somewhere, out of space itself. It was brief, but it was immense. It shook the nest. It overloaded the frequencies of their vox-systems for a moment. It hurt their ears.

Slaughter's visor display took a moment to reboot.

'What in Throne's name was that?' he asked.

'Contacting the fleet,' reported Frenzy. 'Checking.'

'Some kind of transmission,' said Chokehold. 'Ultra-high frequency. Gross intensity. Duration six point six seconds. A new weapon, perhaps?'

'Perhaps,' said Slaughter grudgingly.

They resumed their advance. After a few minutes, fleet tactical reported back that they hadn't been able to identify the sound either. It had been picked up by Imperial forces all across the planet, and in orbit too.

'A new weapon,' muttered Chokehold. 'I told you...'

There was another burst about half an hour later, duration seven point nine seconds. By then, Slaughter's force was locked in a furious hand-to-hand war with dozens of veterans. The noise took them all by surprise.

When it ended, the Chrome veterans were slightly stunned, and then recommitted to the fight with renewed fury. As though they were afraid, and starting to panic.

# SIX

## Ardamantua

The magos biologis' name was Phaeton Laurentis. When the first noise burst occurred he was preparing to enter the blisternest behind the shield-corps advance. The blast of sound terminally damaged two of his six sensitive, audio-specialised servitors. Like Slaughter, he immediately contacted fleet tactical, and also sent direct vox-burst communiques to the staff of his own vessel, the survey barge *Priam*, which was in the vanguard of the Imperial Fists fleet.

'Tell them I need at least a dozen more audio-drones shipped to the surface,' he told his communication servitor. The servitor, a grinning bronze skull mounted on a cloak-swathed wire anatomy, chattered its teeth mechanically as its brainstem fired processed vox data-packets into the aether. Laurentis reeled off a list of other complex devices he would need: techno-linguistic engines, parsing cogitators, vocalisation monitors, trans-aetheric responder coils.

'Permission denied for surface drop of requested material,'

the communication servitor replied after a minute. Its voice, which emanated from a mesh speaker cone fused into its verdigrised collarbone, was oddly that of a young woman. As the voice spoke, the bronzed skull clacked its teeth aimlessly and uselessly.

'On what authority?' asked Laurentis, offended.

'Undertaking Command,' the servitor replied.

'Open me a direct link with the Chapter Master,' said Laurentis.

'Pending.'

'Of course, he will be busy. Inform me when the link is open,' Laurentis said, and strode off to mount one of the motorised carts that would convey, on their heavy, clattering treads, the magos' survey staff into the alien habitat.

Smoke from the nest clambered into the sky as if trying to flee the warzone. The heavens above were black with filth, and embers rained down. Around the edges of the nest, which were cracked and splintered like the shell of an egg, the soil and vegetation were awash with draining bio-fluids from ruptured nest organics and the ichor of slain Chromes. There was a pervasive stink of rotten fruit.

Such a sight, such a vivid display of an alien ecology, even one so damaged and desecrated, should have filled Magos Biologis Laurentis with total fascination. His life had been dedicated to the study of xenoforms, and it was very rare, even for a man as distinguished and respected as he was, to see such a spectacle first hand. Usually, the only traces of hostile xenoforms and their habitats that magi biologis got to inspect were burned scraps and fused tissue residues brought back by undertaking fleets.

However, his enthusiasm for his research, and the alien specimens spread out before him awaiting his probes and scalpels, was muted. The sound had bothered him, and he knew exactly why.

A total of four noise bursts, each of progressively longer duration, occurred in the following ninety minutes. After the fourth, Chapter Master Cassus Mirhen walked slowly and thoughtfully across the gleaming bridge space of the battle-barge *Lanxium*, took his seat on the great steel throne, and gestured to the vox-servitor that had been waiting patiently for almost two hours.

The command crew and the bridge officers watched the Chapter Master anxiously. He was a great man, arguably the greatest warrior alive in the Imperium. His deeds and achievements were recognised on an honour roll that was the envy of all other Chapter Masters. He was commander of the Imperial Fists, and the living embodiment of Dorn himself.

*But he had a temper, oh yes indeed...*

Since the latest phase of the attack had begun in the early part of the day, Mirhen had been on his feet in the ship's strategium, watching every last scrap of data as it came through from air and ground forces, and taking personal control of every tactical nuance. Defence was the Imperial Fists' greatest skill, and even in attack, the Chapter's strategy was reflective and complex. Nothing was left to chance. Nothing was over-extended or risked. Leave the headlong insanity of assault to the likes of the Fenrisian Wolves or the White Scars. The Imperial Fists were the Imperium's

DAN ABNETT

finest military technicians, and even the most fluid plans of assault were made with the same precision reserved for indefatigable defence. It was often repeated that the Lion had once scoffed at Dorn's precision thinking, remarking that 'no plan ever survives contact with the enemy,' to which Dorn had retorted, 'Then you're not making the right plans.'

Indeed, Imperial Fists methodology, the methodology that had saved Terra in its darkest hour, the methodology espoused by Rogal Dorn and inherited by Mirhen, seldom used the word 'plan.' Mirhen prided himself on 'schemes of attack,' whereby layers of careful, preconsidered variables could be stripped back as necessary. Every step of combat – that most chaotic and mercurial of all circumstances in the galaxy – gave way to multiple possibilities. Some warriors, especially the noble Ultramarines, reacted intuitively to such possibilities as they occurred.

An Imperial Fist identified and prepared for all of them, and simply diverted to the part of the scheme that was most appropriate.

Most believed that Mirhen's presence in the strategium, and his hands-on approach to the Ardamantua Undertaking, was typical of this obsessive precision thinking. In truth, Mirhen liked the challenge. War did not come often enough for him. It was a test, a game, an exercise, a trial. He wanted to be involved, entirely involved; he wanted to push himself.

War was fading away in the Imperium of Mankind. The purposes for which the likes of the Adeptus Astartes had been engineered were dying out. They had done their job. Peace prevailed across a billion worlds. Only distant skirmishes and half-hearted wars boiled along the hem of the frontier, most of them the endless campaigns of suppression against the ubiquitous greenskins. The orks never went away. They menaced and harried the edges of the Imperium like packs of feral dogs, and every now and then broke in through the metaphorical fence and got at the metaphorical livestock. Once or twice every few centuries, a new and potent bestial warboss arose, their numbers multiplied in response, and another of their mass onslaughts was unleashed. Mirhen knew from intelligence briefings that the greenskins were currently enjoying one of these periodic revivals, and that for the last few decades some of the frontier wars had been especially hot. But even so, they were exactly that – *frontier* wars. They were very far away, far too far to act as effective demonstrations of Imperial might to the population of the Terran Core. And the orks had not been a serious, palpable threat since they had been stopped at Ullanor by the beloved Emperor Himself.

Ardamantua was different. It wasn't the frontier, it was close. It was a genuine xenos threat without being a critical one. It was also an opportunity to live-test the capabilities of his Chapter and his own mind, and to demonstrate the enduring worth of the Adeptus Astartes. Opportunities on the scale of Ardamantua were all too rare.

Mirhen's temper was famous. It manifested, more often than not, when those around him failed to keep pace with his tactical thought process. He'd even been known to rage at cogitators and data-engines. His anger showed when the rest of the universe failed to stay in step with his brilliance.

First Captain Algerin had privately remarked that Mirhen had become Chapter Master *because* of his anger. Yes, his tactical genius was astonishing, but it was equalled by three dozen of the senior ranking Fists. What Mirhen had was a tactical genius tempered by passion and the unpredictability of gut feeling. Some said there was more of Sigismund in him than Dorn.

When Mirhen retired to his throne during the pitch of the assault, all of the bridge crew expected his anger to emerge. The noise bursts had confounded them and there was a tense feeling that they represented something that had not been factored into a precondition.

'Connect me,' the Chapter Master told the vox-servitor.

The servitor extended its vox-speakers and opened its mouth. A beam of light projected out of it and formed a hololithic image on the deck at the Chapter Master's feet.

A jumping, inconstant pict image of the magos biologis appeared, cut and broken by atmospherics and data-feed. Laurentis was in profile and appeared to be riding on some kind of open vehicle, and the light conditions were poor.

'Magos,' said Mirhen.

'Sir,' the magos crackled back over the speakers. He turned to look at his pict unit, his face turning full on in the image.

'You sent a signal?'

'Over two hours ago, sir. I need to transport equipment to the surface from my vessel, and permission has been denied.'

'There is an assault underway, magos. I was not in a position to grant orbit to surface passage for any non-military transport.'

'Are you now in a position to authorise my request?' asked the magos. 'If I can explain, I need the items so I can–'

'You don't need to explain, magos,' said Mirhen.

'I don't?'

'It concerns these bursts of noise, doesn't it?' asked the Chapter Master. 'Your comm-request came through very shortly after the first one. You have not got in my way before, magos. It was slow-witted of me not to realise that you would only request a surface drop in the middle of an action like this if it was both urgent and pertinent.'

'I appreciate the compliment, sir. You are quite correct.'

'Tell me what you know,' said Mirhen.

'I believe the sound is organic in origin.'

'Organic?' asked the Chapter Master. 'On this scale? Magos, it was a global detection–'

'Organic, though it may have been synthesised and boosted,' Laurentis replied. 'I cannot explain why I feel this to be the case. I hope you will trust my experience and judgement. Both of those things tell me it is organic.'

'A bio-weapon? Something the Chromes have that we haven't predicted?'

The holo-image of Laurentis shook its head.

'I think it is communication, sir,' he said. 'We just have to work out what it is saying. Hence my request for additional equipment.'

'Your transport is already underway at my order,' said Mirhen.

'Thank you, sir.'

'Are you suggesting the Chromes are trying to communicate with us? Since mankind first encountered them, they have not shown any propensity for sentient communication.'

'This attack may have pushed them to a level where they

feel communication is necessary, sir,' replied Laurentis. 'Perhaps they have broken their long silence because they are desperate to sue for peace or surrender. I cannot answer that yet, but I believe it's clear that *something* is trying to communicate.'

'Stay on this link, magos,' Mirhen said. 'I want to hear more about this, and I want to be apprised as soon as–'

He broke off as the pict image of Laurentis became choppy. The magos appeared to be agitated. There were flashes of light, and a great deal of background noise and interference. The image started to jump and wink out.

Then it shut off altogether.

'Reconnect!' Mirhen roared. 'Reconnect that link!'

'Transmission disrupted at source, sir,' the servitor reported.

'I think the magos' party has come under attack,' said Third Captain Akilios, awaiting his master's orders.

'I can damn well see that,' said Mirhen. 'Route the nearest available ground forces to him immediately. Pull his fat out of the fire. I need him alive.'

# SEVEN

## Ardamantua

Claws. They were definitely claws. They weren't 'digital blades affixed to or articulated from forelimbs', which was a phrase Laurentis was pretty sure he'd used several times in the genotype description he'd composed for the Chromes.

They were claws.

It was perfectly straightforward to see them as such when they were swinging at you.

The Chrome was massive. It was one of the darker-hued forms, one of the new ones that Laurentis had overheard a great deal of vox-traffic about once the Adeptus Astartes had entered the blisternest.

He'd been dying to see one.

How ironic.

It must have weighed about five hundred kilos. Its hard-shelled back was ridged, with a pronounced, sclerotic-looking hump. The shoulder portions and upper joints were bound with layers of muscle and sinew, like a great simian. The face... The face was not a face. It was a knot of ocular organs on the snout of the armoured head-crest, surmounting a powerful set of chattering mouthparts. The sound it made – *clack-clack-clack* – was like some funereal march, like a death-drum, like rot-beetles clicking away in wood.

The Chrome warrior-form had come out of a side aperture in the nest tunnel and attacked the leading carts in the magos biologis' convoy. One cart was already mangled, and the curving tunnel walls were spattered with blood and lubricant fluid from three servitors that had been dismembered in the first strike.

'Warrior-form' was the word the Imperial Fists were using. It was a perfectly apt term, simple and technically appropriate. The creature was combat adapted. It was built for fighting. It was not, like the regular Chromes, a worker or drone obliged to defend the nest.

Gun servitors in Laurentis' retinue had already opened fire, but their lasweapons were not sufficiently powerful to wound the armoured hulk. It came forwards, wrenching a second cart into the air, spilling its occupants, tipping it.

The confines of the tunnel were so tight. There was nowhere to run, to move to, no air to breathe. The light was poor and gunfire was causing intense visual disturbance. Everyone was shouting. Las-shots howled. Laurentis could hear the voice of the comm-servitor as it tried to reconnect his link with the Chapter Master.

He was caught up in it. It was exactly where he didn't want to be, exactly where he'd spent his career trying not to be. He was caught in the untameable insanity of combat.

'Save yourself, magos,' the pilot servitor beside him said in a flat and oddly sad tone. Hardwired and bone-bonded into the cart's driving position, the servitor itself could hardly escape. Even so, Laurentis wanted to snarl in outrage. Save himself? How? Where could he run to? Up the tunnel, away from the survey convoy? Into the nest, alone?

There was a sharp bang. The warrior-form had ploughed into one of the gun servitors, its claws ripping open the plated bio-organic torso like chisels. Power cables shredded and the servitor's power plant exploded, showering sparks and sizzling fragments and releasing a stink of ozone.

Brain-dead, transfixed by the claws, the gun servitor went into a death-shock spasm, its autonomic systems reacting mindlessly, ungoverned by any programmed control protocols.

The double lasguns mounted onto each of its twitching wrists began to fire, the blue barrels pumping to and fro in their pneumatic sleeves as they spat out bolt after bolt of lethal, shaped light.

The first flurry ripped through three servitors and a biologis assistant standing on the stern of the nearest cart, killing them and making them tumble like skittles. Another wild burst blew out the port-side motivators of the same cart, and then killed two servitors on the ground beside it.

Laurentis flinched as another stray shot whined past, blowing out the head of his cart's pilot servitor. The servitor didn't even slump. The braced and bonded figure remained rigid in its driving socket, smoke streaming from the burned-out bowl of its skull.

Laurentis leapt over the side of the cart, and started to

run up the narrow space between the cart and the tunnel wall. He could hear his comm-servitor, wired to its dedicated function, single-mindedly trying to reconnect his link with the Chapter Master in orbit.

Laurentis found his robes tangled in his feet. He was aware of a hot prickling in his lungs and chest, in his throat. Terror. Panic. He was going to die. He was going to die. Fleeing was the only possible option, but it was pointless. He was going to die.

Behind him, the warrior-form shook the dead gun servitor off its claws and sent the servitor's corpse crashing away, bouncing off the tunnel roof and then the fairing of another cart.

Laurentis ran. He realised he wasn't very good at it. The tunnel floor underneath his feet was spongy and thick with slime or mucus, and his boots weren't in any way the right sort of footgear for these conditions. He banged his elbow on the vector cowling of the cart, and it really hurt. He could feel sweat streaming down his spine. He was hyperventilating. He was about to throw up.

A body flew over his head, hit the tunnel wall with a twig-snap of fracturing bones, went limp and fell at his feet. It was Overseer Finks, the convoy manager. Laurentis recoiled and felt the hot acid of reflux in his throat. He wanted to stop and help his colleague, though the overseer was clearly past helping. He didn't need a Laudex Honorium in Advanced Biologis to know that any human missing quite that much torso probably wasn't alive any more.

It felt squalid, however, squalid and shameful to just step over the man's body. It felt improper to pass by and keep running. But the alternatives, stopping or turning back, seemed even more unfortunate.

Laurentis realised, with a scientist's detached precision, that he had frozen. Fright had conquered flight. He was shutting down.

The cart he had dismounted from, the cart he had been in the process of running past, suddenly overturned and slammed into the side of the tunnel. It deformed and buckled, metal plating and machine components shredding and scattering. It had been half-sheltering him, but now he was alone, a man standing beside a corpse with a curved, slimy wall behind him.

The cart compressed further as the advancing warrior-form pounded it and mashed its structure into the wall. The heavy throb of *clack-clack-clack* welled out of the dark beast's oesophagus. Blood and oil drooled off its claws.

'Golden Throne preserve me,' Laurentis muttered, his voice as quiet as a sub-vox echo.

# EIGHT

## Ardamantua – orbital

Captain Sauber, known as Severance, commander of Lotus Gate Company, cocked his head to one side.

'This isn't the noise bursts?' he asked.

'No, sir,' replied the adept. 'Though they are recurring.'

'We have compiled a list of timings and durations, sir,' added another adept. 'Would you like to review it?'

'No,' said Severance. He kept staring at the cogitator screen, processing the data. 'You're saying this *isn't* the noise bursts?'

'No, sir, a separate phenomenon,' replied the first adept.

'Gravitational?' asked Severance.

'Yes,' said the adept.

'It reminds me of the mass-gravity curve of a Mandeville point,' said Severance.

At his side, Shipmistress Aquilinia clucked her tongue, impressed.

'What?' asked Severance, turning to look at her.

'You recognised a Mandeville curve from a schematic

profile,' said the shipmistress, looking up at him. 'I thought you were just a soldier. That's impressive.'

'The mass-gravity curve is similar to a Mandeville point,' said the adept, 'though of far, far less magnitude–'

'Which makes it all the more impressive that the captain recognised it,' Aquilinia snapped at him.

'Yes, mistress.'

'Can we get to the point?' asked Severance. 'Are we detecting gravitational instabilities in the Ardamantua orbital zone?'

'Slight ones, yes, sir,' said the adept.

'The whole zone was surveyed as we approached,' said Severance.

'These are new,' said the adept.

'Like the noise bursts?' asked Severance.

The adept nodded. 'We noticed the first approximately two minutes after the initial noise burst occurrence. And only then because of a slight drift in our orbital anchor point. Analysis showed that a tiny gravitic anomaly had occurred eighty-eight point seven two units off the port-side drive assembly, causing the anchor-slide. We corrected. Then we scanned, and saw that sixteen other anomalies of similar profile had occurred during the period.'

Severance turned and crossed the long, narrow bridge of the strike cruiser *Amkulon*. It was like the nave of an ancient cathedral, with various function-specific crew departments working in lit galleries stacked on either side above him. Aquilinia hurried after the massive armoured warrior.

'Open a channel to the flagship!' she cried. 'The captain wants voice to voice with the Chapter Master!'

'You read my mind,' said Severance.

'I grasp the significance,' she replied. 'If there's genuine, previously undetected gravitational instability in the orbital zone, we will have to back the fleet out. That would seriously compromise the ground assault.'

Severance nodded. He felt cheated. His wall wasn't even deployed yet. His men were prepped and ready in the drop holds of the *Amkulon*.

'Did you see them?' he growled at Aquilinia. 'The gravity blips, popping up like blisters, and then closing again. Have you seen that before?'

She shook her head.

'I've seen gravity fraying close to major mass giants,' she said. 'And you get that kind of peppering, blistering effect on the fringes during translation in and out of the empyrean.'

'Hence the similarity to a Mandeville profile?'

'Exactly. Throne's sake, captain, I've seen plenty of non-Euclidian gravity effects on the rip-curve of the translation interface. Daemon space does not behave itself, as my mentors used to say.'

'But you think this is natural?'

She shrugged. A brass-framed optic slid down from her crested headdress, spearing data-light into her left eye so she could review the adept's findings again.

'I believe so. Yes, yes. It has to be. There's no patterning. We have to accept we've entered a gravitationally unstable zone.'

'I'll inform the Chapter Master,' said Severance.

He took the proffered speaker horn in his huge left hand and waited a moment for the vox-servitor to cue him that connection was established.

DAN ABNETT

'Speak,' said Mirhen's voice over the link.

'Severance, Lotus Gate, *Amkulon*,' said Severance. 'We're plotting increasing gravitational instability in the upper and outer orbital zone, sir. Routing all data to your bridge.'

He looked at Aquilinia, who nodded and began issuing orders to her data-adepts.

'You should be receiving data now, sir,' Severance began.

The deck shuddered. There was a dull, heavy sound of something vast and leaden colliding with something of equal mass. Hot, acrid smoke gusted across the bridge.

Alarms started to sound.

'What was that?' Severance asked.

The shipmistress was already yelling commands and requesting clarification. Bridge personnel dashed to their stations.

'*Amkulon*? Severance, report.' Mirhen's voice scratched out of the vox-speakers.

'Stand by,' Severance replied. He looked at the shipmistress.

'A gravity pocket spontaneously opened in our starboard reactor core,' she said. 'We're ruptured and venting. I don't know if we can contain the damage and maintain our position.'

'There must be–' Severance began.

'Captain, please get your company and all auxiliaries off this ship now,' said Aquilinia, 'before we suffer catastrophic anchor-point failure and nosedive into that planet.'

# NINE

## Terra – the Imperial Palace

The Senatorum session had lasted for almost seven hours. Tedium had been etched on some faces by the time it drew to a close, and few had been able to disguise their dissatisfaction when Ekharth had announced that they would resume after a three-hour interval as there were still eighty-seven items remaining on the agenda.

Vangorich withdrew to his private suite to rest his mind. The problem as he saw it, and he believed he saw it very clearly, was that the instrument of governance was not as sharp as it had once been. The Old Twelve had met regularly, and had dealt specifically with high-order matters. Everything else had been delegated to the lower tiers of government and the Administratum. Any review of the parliamentary records showed how economically and concisely the Senatorum had dealt with state affairs in previous, greater ages. Greater ages, populated by greater men.

Now the Senatorum was bloated and fat, over-stuffed with hangers-on and minor officials, and it met on a whim, whenever Udo or any of the other core members felt that it should. Business piled up, most of it far too trivial to bother the dignity of a proper Senatorum. And as for the actual process! These people weren't politicians. Procedure trudged along. No one knew how to debate properly. The most mindless committee vote took forever. At every touch and turn, the in-fighting and rivalries between the High Twelve spewed out and gnawed like acid into the gears of government, slowing everything down.

The decision taken on isotope shipments, for example. Utterly ridiculous. They had actually voted through a policy that would actively harm the Imperium by retarding the efficiency of shipbuilding in the Uranic shipyards. Did anyone dare see it that way? Of course not! Mesring had wanted the vote swayed to protect his family's huge commercial interests in the Tang Sector, and he had called in favours from those in his power bloc. House Mesring had benefited. The Imperium had not.

Vangorich's suite was quiet. His signet ring deactivated the pain door and rested the alarm systems. He went inside. The outer room was panelled in dark oak, and lined with couches dressed in gleaming black leather upholstery. On a lit display stand ancient fragments of pottery, pre-dating the Golden Age of Technology, hung in suspension fields.

Vangorich put down his data-slate and a sheaf of documents, and walked to the sideboard to pour an amasec. The drinks, a modest collection of fine marks, were kept in special, tamper-proof bottles. He sniffed the empty glass for residue before he poured. Old habits.

Before he took his first sip, he used his thumb ring to deactivate a secret drawer in the top of the sideboard cabinet, slid it open, and took out the elegant, long-barrelled plasma pistol cushioned inside.

Without looking around, he said, 'The left-hand armoire, beside the De Mauving landscape.'

Then he turned and aimed the weapon at the item of furniture he had just described.

A small but powerfully built man in a black bodyglove stepped out from behind the armoire and nodded sheepishly to Vangorich.

'Nice try,' said Vangorich, and lowered the weapon.

'Every time, sir,' said the man. 'What was it on this occasion?'

'Body-heat sensors,' said Vangorich, taking a sip of his drink.

'I deactivated them.'

Vangorich nodded.

'And, therefore,' he said, 'I got no body-heat notifications from the security overwatch when I entered the suite, not even my own.'

'Ah,' said the man, slightly ashamed.

'Also, you managed to throw a slight side-shadow under the foot of the armoire. You didn't take into account the glow-globes to your left.'

The man nodded, chastened.

'Where is she?' asked Vangorich.

'The atrium, sir,' said the man.

Vangorich poured a second amasec and carried both drinks through to the small inner courtyard. Wienand was

sitting on the bench beside the thermal pool, watching the luminous fish dart in the steaming shallows.

'All done humiliating my bodyguard?' she asked, not getting up.

'A visit from you wouldn't be the same without an opportunity to humiliate your man,' he replied, handing her one of the glasses.

'Kalthro is very good,' she said, 'the best we have. You're the only person who ever catches him out.'

'I consider it to be part of his education, a gift from the Officio Assassinorum to the Inquisition.'

He sat down next to her and crossed one knee over the other, rocking his glass.

'Your visits are less frequent these days, Wienand,' he said. 'I was beginning to think you didn't like me. To what do I owe this pleasure?'

'Agenda item 346,' she said.

'346?' He paused and thought for a second, running through the day's fearsome data-load in his eidetic memory. 'The Imperial Fists' undertaking to Ardamantua?'

'Yes,' she said.

'It was the quickest item of the day. It was raised and covered in about two minutes. Pending, awaiting reports from the Chapter Master.'

Wienand nodded. Her cheekbones were as sharp as glacial cliffs. Her hair was silver in the light.

'What of it, Wienand?'

She pursed her lips.

'A threat is developing,' she said.

'A threat?'

'In the opinion of the Inquisition, yes.'

'A xenos threat?'

She nodded.

'They're called... Chromes, aren't they?' asked Vangorich. 'I did see the briefing paper.'

'The Imperial Fists have undertaken the mission to Ardamantua to suppress a xenoform outbreak. The xenoforms are known as Chromes.'

He raised his eyebrows.

'What am I missing?' he asked.

'You tell me.'

Vangorich shrugged. 'I don't know. As I understand it, these Chromes are like vermin. Nothing out of the ordinary. They have to be dealt with. I gather their numbers are greater than usual. The Fists have mobilised in prodigious numbers, almost full force. I understood that was a political gesture, to show them being useful in peacetime.'

He hesitated.

'Wienand, if it's a threat that seriously jeopardises an almost full-strength Chapter, you're starting to worry me.'

She cleared her throat.

'No, the politics should worry you,' she said.

'Go on.'

'Mirhen's taken pretty much his entire Chapter to Ardamantua to deal with the xenos threat. He's the only one taking it seriously.'

'And why is he taking it seriously? Who alerted him to it?'

'We did,' she said.

'Of course you did.'

'The Fists are more than capable of dealing with the

Chrome problem,' Wienand said. 'The point is, they shouldn't have to. The Imperium should be meeting the challenge. Ardamantua should have been a joint undertaking between the Astra Militarum and the Navy, with a backbone of Fists as its cutting edge. Deploying the whole Chapter was ungainly and clumsy.'

'Heth should–'

'Heth can't commit Guard forces without the cooperation of the Navy, and Lansung is more interested in the glory wars against the pathetic greenskins on the frontier. That's where he's sending his fleets. He's fighting border wars and claiming territory practically in his own name. And with Udo backing him, he's pretty much got a free hand to do that.'

'Like too many seats on the council, Lansung places his own interests above those of the Imperium,' said Vangorich.

She nodded again.

'Ardamantua is just six warp-weeks from Solar Approach. It's not a frontier war. It's on our doorstep.'

'And?'

'We've been intercepting comm-traffic between the undertaking fleet and the Chapter House. In the last ten hours, relative, problems have begun to arise. We anticipate that Mirhen will be forced to request support and reinforcement inside a week.'

'Against a xenos threat? Against... *vermin*?'

She held up a hand.

'He will need it. And Lansung won't give it. We must make sure we apply pressure today.'

'Pressure?'

Wienand's soft smile tightened.

'Mirhen may have underestimated the nature of the xenos threat.'

'Since when did the Imperial Fists underestimate anything?' asked Vangorich.

'Since, I think, they were forced to act without the combined support of the Senatorum,' she replied. 'I believe – that is to say that the strategic planners at the Inquisition, and my immediate superiors, believe – that the Imperial Fists will require direct fleet support within the next three months in order to complete the undertaking.'

'Or?'

'Or the xenos threat could actually threaten the Terran Core.'

Vangorich thought about that.

'There hasn't been a threat inside the Core for... centuries,' he said lightly, much more lightly than he was feeling. 'Xenos or otherwise. It's unthinkable.'

'Politics could make it happen. Power play.'

He considered her carefully.

'These... *Chrome* things? Really? That dangerous?'

'We believe there is a palpable and credible xenos threat. We brought it to the attention of Udo, Lansung, Kubik and Mirhen as a Critical Situation Packet. Only Mirhen agreed on its credibility.'

'What aren't you telling me, Wienand?'

'Nothing, Drakan. Nothing at all.'

She fixed him with eyes as chilly as starlight.

'It's the principle of this matter. Personal ambition is allowing the Senatorum to become weak and inefficient.

This is a matter we have discussed before. Now it threatens to become more than a theoretical annoyance. I will not stand by and see a core world burned or overrun just to demonstrate the fatal inadequacies of the Senatorum.'

'What are you proposing?' he asked.

'We bring the issue into special business. Lansung, Mesring and Udo are too strong, and too many look to them, even if we swing Heth with us. Zeck too, perhaps, because the reputation of the Adeptus Astartes is at stake and he holds them in especial regard. The point is, we don't try to change the world overnight. All we want is the Senatorum to recognise the problem, and get Heth to propose a fifty-regiment reinforcement expedition to back up the undertaking. We basically shame Lansung into approving fleet support. The Lord High Admiral does not want to go down on the parliamentary record as the man who refused support and left the core worlds wide open.'

'Can he commit what we need? If we embarrass the man, we could corner him.'

'I've reviewed it,' she replied, 'carefully. There are three Segmentum quarter-fleets he could mobilise easily enough, or two vanguard attack squadrons standing off Mars. He has the resources. Thank Throne, he hasn't sent them all to the frontier.'

Vangorich sat back and watched the fish dart about.

'Let's not make it a hard vote,' he said.

'How so?'

'Let's not push him or humiliate him into compliance. Let's make the case and give Lansung the opportunity to look magnanimous.'

'You let him be the hero of the hour?'

'Does that matter if the Terran Core is protected? Let's give him the opportunity to look good in the eyes of the Senatorum and the populace. Let him take it as a win. Wienand, you get much more out of people if you let them feel good about doing what you want them to do.'

She laughed.

'And if he does not?'

'Then we apply pressure. Then we threaten him with shame. You have my vote. I have a little sway with Zeck, and I believe I can call in a favour owed by Gibran if necessary.'

'Good,' she said.

'Good,' he replied, smiling. 'I like our little talks.'

She rose to her feet and handed him her empty glass.

'This xenos threat, Wienand,' he asked. 'Really, what aren't you telling me?'

'I'm telling you everything,' she said.

'I see.' He shrugged. 'When will you allow me to know your forename, Wienand?'

'My dear Drakan, what makes you think you even know my surname? Killing is your business, sir. Secrets are ours.'

# TEN

## Ardamantua

The warrior-form came at Laurentis, jaws open, ropes of saliva stretched out between the points of laterally extended biting parts.

A force knocked it aside. The creature was smashed to the magos biologis' right, splashing into the muddy slime that drooled along the tunnel floor. The impact that felled it was like the concussion of a demolition tool-bit working rockcrete.

The huge beast couldn't get up. Something had it pinned. A humanoid form in yellow: an Imperial Fist.

A captain. Laurentis could see the rank marks, despite the wash of gore and mud plastering the Space Marine's armour.

Slaughter. It was Slaughter.

Slaughter had brought the Chrome down, floored it and pinned it by the throat with his left fist. The Space Marine's right fist was a piston, ramming a huge combat knife into the Chrome's distended belly over and over again. Something burst. Brown liquid sprayed out across the tunnel.

Laurentis recoiled from the vented reek of formic acid and rancid milk.

The warrior-form went slack. Slaughter got off it, but his combat knife was wedged between the integuments of its armour. A second large xenos thundered down the tunnel on the heels of the first, trailing the semi-articulated pieces of a driving servitor from one of its limbs.

Slaughter abandoned his combat knife. Leaving it embedded in the torso of his first kill, he threw himself over the corpse and into the face of the second warrior-form. He drew his broadsword as he leapt, sweeping the powered blade out of its over-shoulder scabbard and forwards, so that its cutting edge led the way.

Space Marine and Chrome warrior-form met. The clash made an air-slap that hurt Laurentis' ears. The Chrome smacked Slaughter hard, twice, its claws drawing sparks off his armour. The Space Marine rocked, reeled back from the blows, and then renewed his efforts, hefting the blade into the Chrome's shoulder with both hands.

It was the Chrome's turn to reel. It staggered sideways. Taking a better grip on his gore-slick sword, Slaughter delivered a second blow that did significantly more damage. Split open, the Chrome tilted and fell backwards.

Laurentis hadn't even seen the third enemy. Slaughter had. The warrior-form was very dark, the colour of a bruise. It came down the tunnel from the other direction, moving with extraordinary speed, claw-limbs hinged out to rain lethal downstrokes on the Imperial Fist.

Slaughter switched around to meet it, hacked with his sword, and took off one forelimb. The creature milled at him, claws glinting in the noxious light. Slaughter ducked aside, letting the blow go long over his shoulder guard, stooping his back into a turn that took him under the Chrome's guard and into its chest. He stabbed his sword in, tip-first, cracking the organic armour, and then shoulder-barged the clacking alien backwards, freeing his blade so he could thrust it again. The second time it went clean through the creature.

He ripped the sword out, and the warrior-form went down.

'Magos?' Slaughter called out, checking up and down the tunnel, sword ready.

'Yes, captain?'

'Are you alive there?'

'I am, captain.'

'Get ready to move with me when I tell you. The Chapter Master has sent Daylight Wall to get you out of this.'

'It is very much appreciated,' said Laurentis. 'I thought I was d–'

'Shhhh!' Slaughter warned him.

From the distance, Laurentis could hear the sound of bolt-weapons firing.

'There's a lot of opposition in this zone,' Slaughter said. 'A lot.'

Laurentis began to wonder where the rest of Daylight Wall Company had got to.

'Let's move,' said Slaughter, and beckoned the magos biologis after him. The captain had made some kind of assessment presumably based on the data his armour was feeding him and incoming vox-signals, neither of which Laurentis was privy to.

They began to work their way back down the nest tunnel, picking their way through the ruins of the magos biologis's convoy. The carriages were all shredded and crushed. His servitors and juniors were dead or fled. Blood-smoke wafted in the gloom of the tunnel. *Now our matter is vaporised,* Laurentis thought unhappily.

'They have shown unexpected resolve within the perimeters of their nest,' he said.

Slaughter grunted in reply.

'We don't much like the unexpected,' the captain said.

'Because?'

'Because nothing should be unexpected.'

'I see.'

'I didn't expect to run out of bolt-rounds today, for example,' Slaughter said. Laurentis saw that the Space Marine captain's massive firearm was clamped to his belt. He'd exhausted its munition supply. The fight must have been extraordinarily intense.

Slaughter glanced down at Laurentis.

'There are supposed to be munition trains moving into the nest, at least one near here,' he added.

'Ah, so that's what I owe my salvation to,' Laurentis replied, trying to sound brave. 'You were looking for the ammunition.'

'I had an order,' snapped Slaughter, 'from the Chapter Master.'

'Of course. I apologise.'

'The fact that you were near a munition train was simply a bonus.'

Laurentis managed a laugh. Then he realised something

that chilled him. Just as Laurentis had done, the Space Marine captain was trying to make light of the situation.

They really were in the most terrible trouble.

# ELEVEN

## Ardamantua – orbital

Chapter Master Cassus Mirhen watched the stricken *Amkulon* begin to fall out of fleet formation. There was something significantly wrong with the strike cruiser's engines. It was venting radioactive clouds and all contact had been lost in a blizzard of vox-interference.

'Did Lotus Gate get clear?' he asked.

Akilios shook his head.

'We don't know yet, sir.'

'Find out as soon as you can. I don't see any drop-pods or escape boats.'

The truth was, it was hard to see much of anything. The incoming feed to the main viewers and the repeater and image-booster screens was fogged by the radiation back-wash and some kind of gravimetric distortion. That was what Severance had been trying to warn them about. Mirhen had most of the *Lanxium*'s tech-staff working on the issue, analysing the data sent over from the *Amkulon*. Initial reports were bad. Pockets of gravity distortion were being detected in a range of orbital locations. No one could explain it, and no one could adequately explain why there had been no sign of the phenomenon before the fleet moved into its assault anchor.

Now there was the *Amkulon* itself. A whole ship, a good ship, and a whole wall of shield-corps brothers, potentially lost.

Mirhen watched the flickering, jumping screen image. The majestic strike cruiser was making a slow, pitching descent into Ardamantua's gravity field, unable to support its mass. How long? An hour? Two? Four? The crippled drives would probably blow out because of the stress before that.

'Can we get relief boats out to them?' he asked.

'We're trying now, sir,' replied Akilios.

'We must be able to fetch some of them off it.'

'Yes, sir.'

Mirhen turned to the ranks of the technicians and science adepts.

'I want this explained,' he said. 'I want this accounted for and explained.'

The adepts nodded, but Mirhen felt no confidence in their response. They were as mystified as he was.

He was about to add further encouragement – at least, what he felt was encouragement – when the bank of screens behind him lit up brightly for a moment.

'What was that?' he asked, turning. 'Was that the *Amkulon*?'

The airwaves were filled with vox-static and ugly distortion.

'No, sir,' replied a detection officer. 'That wasn't the *Amkulon*. Sir, the battle-barge *Antorax* just... just exploded, sir.'

# TWELVE

## Ardamantua

The sky was weeping light.

Slaughter kicked his way through a half-collapsed section of tunnel wall and hauled himself onto the softly curving upper surface of the blisternest.

It was raining some kind of liquid that wasn't water through an ugly squall that blew sidelong and made every surface slick and sticky. The nest was a huge sprawl, like some mass of offal oozing on a slab, magnified to titanic proportions. There were loops of tunnel that looked like intestinal knots, there were renal lumps and lobed chambers. Some sections of the vast, organic city were patterned coils like the fossil imprint of ancient seashells. Other sections were crushed to pulp by orbital bombardment and airstrikes. Smoke bled up from the blisternest in a thousand places, mixed with the wind, and washed into the squalling storm. Slaughter heard the downpour tick and tap on his helm and armour.

'Come up,' he called.

Cutthroat climbed after him, and then reached down to

haul the dishevelled magos biologis up out of the tunnel. After them came Stab and Woundmaker. Slaughter had left the rest of Daylight Wall inside the nest under Frenzy's command. The Chapter Master's express orders had been to get Laurentis to the contact point. Well, four of them could do that. There was no sense pulling a whole company out. He'd voxed that decision to the *Lanxium*, but he hadn't had a reply. Something was chopping vox and pict to hell. Atmospherics. It was like Karodan Monument all over again. They'd been deaf and blind there.

And they'd still won.

The magos biologis was looking around, blinking at the daylight. The rain ran off his face and plastered his robes to his body.

'What's that?' he asked, pointing at the sky.

'We haven't got time for sight-seeing,' snapped Woundmaker. Woundmaker was a sergeant, a good man. In the last stretch of tunnel, they'd come upon one of the automated munition trains sent in to support them. It had been mangled beyond recognition by Chrome warrior-forms, and the servitors slain, but Woundmaker and Stab had managed to drive the enemy off and recover some reloads for their bolters. He was sorting and distributing them.

'No, look,' said Laurentis.

Slaughter took the four clips Woundmaker handed him and turned to look where the magos biologis was pointing. There was a light in the sky. It was a broad, diffuse light, weeping out of the ugly cloud cover, but there was a malicious little glowing coal at the heart of it, small and red, like the ember-fragment of a star.

'That's a ship death,' said Cutthroat bluntly.

Slaughter heard Woundmaker curse. He'd been too ready to dismiss the magos biologis' comment, but he could see that Cutthroat was right. They could all see he was right. They'd all seen a ship die from planetside. It was a heart-breaking thing.

'When in Throne's name did these vermin get orbital weapons?' asked Woundmaker. 'When did they get ship-to-ship capability?'

'We still don't know precisely how the Chromes distribute themselves across space,' said Laurentis. 'It is presumed they employ some form of pod or seed dispersal via fluctuations in the warp, but a full scale migration of the magnitude that would explain their population density here has never been witnessed or described. We don't believe they have what we would consider to be ships or a fleet, no vessels at all, but–'

He fell silent. Four angular visors glared at him, rain beading off their beaked jaws.

'I... I'm just saying,' Laurentis managed. 'I don't know how the Chromes could have taken out one of our ships. Perhaps it is an unhappy coincidence, or an accident.'

'There are no coincidences!' Stab told him.

Cutthroat began to say something about accidents and defaming the ability of the fleet.

'Well, something's happened,' said Slaughter, cutting them both off. 'That's a dead ship up there, and a big one too. The magos is right. If the Chromes couldn't hit it, that leaves accident, or coincidence. And coincidence means–'

'What?' asked Laurentis.

'Someone else,' said Slaughter.

A noise burst filled the air. Outdoors, in the stinking open air, it was like the booming of a warhorn, the braying of some daemonic voice. The air seemed to shudder. All four Imperial Fists winced as it stripped through their helmet vox-systems and assaulted their ears. Laurentis felt it prickle his skin. The hairs on his arm rose, despite the rain. Static. Ozone. Around the distant, broken steeples at the blister-nest heart, chain lightning flickered and crackled in a sickly yellow display. Two more noise bursts followed. Laurentis felt the actual structure of the blisternest beneath them resonate with the plangent sound.

'The Chromes are capable of a great deal more than we realise,' Laurentis told his guardians. 'These noises... these bursts of noise... They are why your Chapter Master has charged you to protect me. I have a theory–'

'Tell us,' said Slaughter bluntly.

Laurentis nodded and shrugged.

'I will, sir. I think it's communication. I think the Chromes are trying to communicate with us. We understood them to be non-sapient animals, but we may have been very wrong about that. I wish to test the communication theory, and that is why I need to get to the drop-point to access specialist equipment.'

Slaughter nodded. He checked the auspex mounted across his left forearm.

'Tracking the drop. It'll be down at DZ 457 in the next twenty minutes. Let's move.'

They started off, crossing the oddly ridged humps and rain-slick gullies of the blisternest's upper surface. The Fists, with their strength, long stride and armoured feet, had no trouble negotiating the unpleasant material. Laurentis kept slipping and slithering. He was wet, and cold to the bone. Woundmaker kept picking him up by the scruff of his robes and setting him back on his feet as if he were some clumsy toddler.

'The point of the communication,' said Laurentis, out of breath and struggling to keep up. 'I mean, the point I was making was that if the Chromes are capable of communication, if they are capable of language, then they may be capable of much else besides. They can clearly cross between worlds and star systems in ways we cannot divine. Maybe they can take out ships. Maybe they have potent weapons for void fights.'

'Ships of their own, after all,' said Slaughter.

'Perhaps.'

'If they are capable of communication,' said Slaughter, pausing for a moment to look at the magos biologis. 'If you prove your theory...'

'Yes?'

'What are they trying to say?'

Laurentis paused.

'I first presumed, captain, that they might be trying to negotiate surrender. That was when they seemed to be at our mercy, when their nest seemed to be toppling under assault.'

'And now?'

'Now, I wonder if it might not be a warning. A cry of defiance. A challenge. Now I wonder if they might not be demanding our surrender.'

'Because they are hurting us?'

Laurentis sighed.

'They are, it seems, taking out our starships. They are harrying our ground assault. The successful outcome of this undertaking is not as clear-cut as we first imagined.'

They followed the rim of the nest down, along to the ugly, chordate ridges that pressed like giant finger-bones into the mud of the river's edge. The noise bursts continued to bark across the smoke-wrapped distances, causing the rain to squall and billow. Laurentis tried to keep a basic log of observable details on his data-slate as he struggled to keep up with his transhuman bodyguards. Fountains of ash and light vomited into the air from regions on the far side of the central blisternest, and the concussive booms reached them a moment later.

'Major munitions,' said Slaughter.

'Orbital strike?' asked Cutthroat.

Woundmaker shook his head.

'Looked like... subterranean.'

'So... our enemy has further weapons we don't know about?' asked Stab.

'That they destroy their own nest with?' asked Cutthroat.

'Don't argue. Don't debate,' Slaughter snapped. 'Get moving.'

Another blast rocked the ground and a huge plume sheeted into the dismal sky six or seven kilometres away. The Fists of Daylight Wall stoically and obediently ignored it and started moving onwards. Laurentis hurried with them.

'It *could* be a new weapon,' conjectured the magos biologis, a little out of breath. 'They might, I suppose... They might destroy their own nest if there was nothing left to be gained from protecting it. It might be... uhm, intended to create confusion and disarray, to take as many of us with them as possible.'

'For what purpose?' asked Slaughter, getting his hand under Laurentis' armpit and frog-marching him over a stretch of mud so slick it was like quicksand.

'If they had a final asset to protect?' Laurentis ventured. 'A queen, or the equivalent? A dominant reproductive female? The egg source? I am just hypothesising, but if the nest was lost, they might destroy it as cover for an evacuation of the queen.'

There was another blast. This one came from much closer at hand. The force of it knocked all five of them over and slapped out a wall of mud and steam. Debris pattered down, and the rain ran brown. The Imperial Fists struggled to their feet. Laurentis coughed and shivered, trying to clear his head.

'My gravitics are shot,' reported Stab, checking his visor display.

'Mine too,' said Cutthroat. 'No, correction. Gravitic register *is* working. It's just showing very irregular patterning.'

'Agreed,' said Stab, 'rechecking. Local gravity just looped for ten milliseconds, and that blast focus was gravitically strong.'

'These weapons... these new weapons...' Slaughter asked. 'They're what? Gravity weapons? Gravity bombs?'

Laurentis struggled to reply. He tried to formulate a reasonable-sounding explanation for why the Chromes should have mastery over gravity, one of the universe's most notoriously uncooperative forces. Maybe their inter-system travel relied on some gravitic drive?

'Watch your heels!' Cutthroat yelled.

Chromes were rushing them from the nest pods behind them. They were standard forms, their silvery shells glinting in the stained light, spattered with mud and liquid, but there were a lot of them. Cutthroat and Stab met the first of them, side-by-side, driving strokes and slices with their hefty blade weapons that sent the xenos tumbling and bouncing backwards, slamming into the ranks behind, slit and spraying. The stink of ichor filled the rain.

Slaughter and Woundmaker got Laurentis back, and began to struggle down the reed-choked slope towards the waterline. The ground, wet as a marsh, was littered with dead xenos from the first phase. Moving backwards, Stab and Cutthroat came after them. Laurentis, gasping with anxiety, marvelled at their bladework. The speed of it. The relentless fury. The precision. Severed pieces of Chromes flew up into the air, spinning. Ichor jetted. The pushing ranks of assaulting xenos stumbled and clambered over the bodies of their dead.

Laurentis had seen ants do that. Forest ants, at the edge of a stream, the first ones drowning and dying so that those behind could use their corpses as a bridge, as a growing bridge.

The ants always got across the stream.

Ants never mourned their dead. They used them.

Another wave of Chromes scurried towards them along the bank to their right, clacking and sounding out the *tek-tek-tek* noise they made with their mouthparts.

Slaughter, positioned on the right, turned to meet them, his broadsword coming out. None of the Space Marines had resorted to bolters. Conservation of munition supplies.

Slaughter's blade met the first Chrome, half-impaled it, then hurled it bodily across the river. It arced and hit the water with a dirty splash. His sword swung back and decapitated the next, and then cleaved the third down the middle through the head.

'Protect the principal!' Slaughter roared.

Laurentis cowered on the mud flats. The four Fists closed in around him, at compass points, each one meeting the assault as it swirled around them from the two lines of attack. There was so much ichor spray in the air that the rain tasted of it. They were all dappled with it. The Chromes threw themselves against the four-point defence, finding only death and dismemberment as a reward for their efforts. *There is nothing*, Laurentis remembered the old saying, *as deadly as an Imperial Fist standing his ground.*

Laurentis wondered how much scrutiny the Masters of the Chapters and other senior minds of the Imperial military, and even the beloved and exalted Emperor Himself when He had set to devising the Legiones Astartes, formulating their minds and bodies... How much scrutiny had they given to natural history, to the behaviour of cooperative animals and insects, to their selfless and almost mechanical efforts? The individual was never important, only the group effect. One quick glance at a magos biologis' notebook or cyclopedia would reveal a thousand examples in nature of selfless cooperation, postlogical stratagems, and ensured survival.

A huge, armoured beetle could easily kill a tiny, lone ant. But the ants always got across the stream.

# THIRTEEN

## Terra – Tashkent Hive

'You look unhappy,' remarked Esad Wire.

'Do I?' replied Vangorich. 'Do I really? You can tell that?'
Wire shook his head.

'No, you can't read that in a face. Not for certain,' he admitted. 'You can't read anything in a face for certain.'

He stared at Vangorich for a moment, Vangorich just standing there in the doorway of the monitor station control room like a shadow brought in by the dusk, and considered him carefully.

'Been a very long time, besides,' Wire added. 'A long time not seeing your face. I'm no longer familiar with its nuances. I wouldn't know what sadness looked like anyway, even if I could read it for sure.'

Wire rose from his worn leather seat, brushing imaginary lint from his double-breasted arbiter jacket.

'A long time,' he said, an echo, spoken only to himself.

Vangorich was still in the doorway. Wire beckoned him.

'You can come in, sir,' he said. 'Come right in. Or do you have to be invited over the threshold like a night ghoul?'

Vangorich stepped inside the control room. It was brightly lit, too brightly lit, the hard shine of the lamp-globes and spots revealing every fatigued edge and scuffed fascia of the control suite: the dials and levers worn by centuries of hands, the milky read-outs, the chattering banks of antiquated switches, the electric noticeboards with their mechanical letters and series lights that stated the day's crimes and actions and, every few minutes, reshuffled and revised, like the journey monitors at transit stations.

Monitor Station KVF (Division 134) Sub 12 (Arbitrator). It had taken Vangorich four hours to get there. An hour's flight east from the Palace by suborbital, then a three-hour descent into the underhives of Tashkent Spire, a journey of rattling lift cages, suspension platforms and dank hallways.

It had taken Esad Wire a great deal longer to reach Monitor Station KVF. After his past life was laundered and washed clean, three years at Adeptus Arbitrator incept training, two more at the Procedural Division in the Asiatic Domes, and then eight years with Tashkent Major Case and another six as a jurisdiction subcommander. Then he got the Sector Overseer star to pin on his jacket, and a monitor control room full of antiquated switches.

Everything was processed, everything formalised. Every crime had to be catalogued and filed, described and posted, and redirected to the appropriate division. It was a ritual-ised system that had never really coped with the actuality of real life and real crime in the vast hive, but it was considered the optimal solution and thus persevered with. Running the data-switching station was also considered a task of great responsibility, and thus always awarded to a man of significance or ability, as a mark of promotion. Esad Wire was not a law enforcer. He did not fight crime. He simply filed it.

The room was essentially automated. Wire made a gesture, and two junior arbiters, the only other living people present, went off to find duties in adjacent chambers.

'"You look unhappy",' said Vangorich. 'After all this time, that's the beginning of your conversation?'

Wire shrugged.

'It struck me as so,' he said.

'How has life treated you since you left the Officio?' Vangorich asked. He did not look at Wire. He studied the chattering, updating lines of tile-type that were rattling up and down the displays.

'One never really leaves the Officio, sir,' Wire replied, with a half-smile.

'No need for the sir,' said Vangorich.

Wire shook his head.

'I think so. You are a man of a certain position in life and the world, and I am another, of another position. The inequality of our states seems to indicate I should call you that.'

'It's good to see you, Beast,' said Vangorich.

'And you, sir.' Wire grinned. 'Damn, I haven't been called that in a long time.'

He walked to the side cupboards and poured two mugs of thick, black caffeine from a jug. He handed one to the Grand Master.

'Social call, is it? Been a couple of decades, about time I visited Esad?'

'I've wanted to before, many times,' said Vangorich with surprising directness. 'Never been appropriate.'

'Is it now?'

'No, but I did it anyway. I needed to get out. I needed to... converse with someone who wasn't anything to do with anything at the Palace.'

'Find a priest,' suggested Wire. 'A confessor.'

'The priests all have agendas,' replied Vangorich.

'So... you're here. Go on.'

'Little men,' said Vangorich, taking a seat at one of the monitor stations and sipping his caffeine. 'Little men, playing at being High Lords. Personal ambition is in danger of costing the Imperium very dearly. I tried to block it, but the Officio doesn't have the clout it once wielded, and I got played.'

'Lansung. Udo. Mesring,' said Wire quietly.

Vangorich smiled.

'Well informed.'

'There's little to do here, sir,' said Wire. 'I fill my time with the data-slates and the court reports. I do like to keep up with the reported business of the legislature and the Senatorum. Politics has always been an interest of mine. My old dad used to say that politics is what determines who lives and who dies, so though the business of parliaments sounds dull, it pays to keep an eye on what those idiots are up to.'

'Published Senatorum records don't show the half of it,' said Vangorich.

'They show enough to see that Lansung's after Lord Commander, and Udo's happy to facilitate that succession. Mesring and Ekharth will go along for the ride and lend their weight, if they get rewarded on the other side. Or is that read too simplistic? Am I just an armchair amateur?'

'Good enough,' said Vangorich. 'It's the usual power play.'

'But?'

'They're so busy playing, they've taken their eyes off the board. The Fists have gone to address the situation, but they'll probably need support. Navy support.'

'The Fists will need support–?' Wire began.

'Let's skip that for now. It's a threat. The Inquisition says so.'

Wire whistled.

'How far out?'

'Far too close. We need the Navy, and we need the Guard, and if we need the Guard, we need the Navy anyway. But Lansung doesn't want to get his toys broken.'

'So make him look good.'

'I tried that,' said Vangorich. 'We brokered a little persuasive block vote to make him commit his fleets, but which allowed him to look like the hero of the hour. And he took it, but he played us. He said that if the Fists needed full support, they should be allowed to commit their entire reserve. He made ships available. Even the wall-brothers have gone from their eternal posts. For the first time ever. The whole Chapter. There isn't an Imperial Fist left on Terra or on the *Phalanx*. It's as if he's handing them glory, as if it's his to give. Of course, by making it possible for the entire Chapter to deploy, he's reduced the commitment of fleet and Guard forces he needs to field.'

'That's not right,' said Esad Wire. 'You don't commit a whole Chapter in one go. That's basic.'

'You do if you're an idiot with dreams of a de facto throne.

You do if you put yourself above the needs of mankind. And you do if you've become so complacent after decades of peace that you think nothing can ever harm us again. Beasts arise.'

Wire laughed, though his face was troubled.

'They do,' he agreed. 'When you least expect. First lesson they ever taught us.'

'And the reason for your nickname,' said Vangorich.

'That belonged to someone else,' said Wire, losing the smile. 'I'm a respectable civil servant now.'

He looked at Vangorich.

'When did this happen?'

'Six weeks ago. It wasn't publicly announced. A matter of security. The reinforcements should reach the main force very soon.'

'*That* close?'

'Oh yes.'

Wire shrugged.

'So, may I ask, sir,' he said, 'what was this visit? An opportunity to vent to a sympathetic ear? Or did you think that I could somehow offer a solution to help an entire Chapter of Adeptus Astartes in trouble?'

Vangorich smiled.

'Back in the day, I would not have put such a task beyond the powers of Beast Krule.'

'Beast Krule's long gone,' said Wire.

Vangorich stood up.

'Anyway, no. Not at all,' he said. 'I don't expect you to have a solution, and we don't need one. It's the entire Chapter of Imperial Fists, plus support, Beast. They will quash this threat very quickly. Very quickly. Then no one will notice or remember how close we came to being stupid.'

He faced Wire.

'That's the real crisis. That's why I came to ask your opinion. It's not what's happening now. What's happening now is an act of strategic idiocy sanctioned by men who are too busy chasing the highest office. It's ugly and ham-fisted, but it will resolve itself, and all will be safe. We can trust the Fists. But in the long term, we are left with men who made it happen, let it happen, and thought it was absolutely fine that it happened. And that presents us with the possibility of what might happen next time, and the time after, and the time after that, until such acts of idiocy really start to cost. These men are not fit, Beast. But they represent a seamless power bloc at the heart of the Twelve that cannot be unshaken or dislodged, even with the most radical tactical voting from the rest of us. The Senatorum Imperialis is theirs and will remain theirs.'

Wire nodded ruefully.

'I came, old friend,' said Vangorich, 'because there is a possibility, with all other options exhausted, that one day soon I might have to ask you to go back to your old job.'

'Glory,' Wire whispered. He took a deep breath. 'I can't go back, sir. Not after all this time... I mean, that's not me any more. I left the Officio...'

Drakan Vangorich looked at him without pity or humour.

'Beasts arise, Esad,' he said. 'And besides, one never really leaves the Officio.'

# FOURTEEN

## Ardamantua – outer system approaches

The translation bells were sounding along the quarterdeck of the *Azimuth*.

Daylight rose to his feet from the arming block, took his helm off the rack, and lowered it over his head. The neck seals hissed and whirred into place.

An attendant approached, dressed in a yellow gown.

'I heard,' said Daylight before the man could speak.

The Imperial Fist methodically placed his bolter in its clamp, selected a gladius and sheathed it, and mag-locked a combat knife to his chestplate. Then he finally adorned his head with the laurel wreath that marked him as the senior Imperial Fist in the reinforcement detachment. The laurel symbol had already been painted on his shoulderplates.

He turned and walked from the arming chamber, out onto the quarterdeck space. Hundreds of attendants in yellow robes stopped and watched him as he strode forwards. It was a moment, a singular moment. Daylight was going to war.

Daylight was aware of the significance. He had longed

for war, and felt guilty for doing so. Only the best were ever given the reward of wall-brother status, but it amounted to a punishment, because it took them from the zones of glory and made them live out their lives on ceremonial sentry duty in the draughty halls of the Palace of Terra.

This had been his dream since he had won the status. Going back to war had been his dream.

Yes, the significance was not lost on him. It was a day full of significance. It was the first time ever that wall-brethren had been allowed to leave Terra and the *Phalanx* and go to war in support of their kind, the first time that the entire Chapter had been committed at one stroke since the days of the Siege, when they had been a Legion still. The first time since then that a capital threat had come inside fifty warp-weeks of the Terran Core.

Though he was a creature bred for war, Daylight was not blind to the political significance either. Attending the Palace as he had done for so many years, he had watched the activities of the Senatorum and knew power play and counter-agendas when he saw them. Daylight's glorious return to war, and the wielding of the Imperial Fists as one unified weapon at this time of crisis, were merely by-products of Lord High Admiral Lansung's ascension. He had made himself look quite imperial by moving his forces in support of the Fists, and even more imperial by magnanimously suggesting that the Fists support and preserve their reputation. He had, in effect, facilitated everything that was happening. The fact that he had effectively sent an entire Chapter of Adeptus Astartes to war left a great deal more unsaid about his power.

Attendants swept up on either side of Daylight and attached a long cloak to his shoulders, a cloak of blue silk that trailed out behind him. Armed footmen fell in step around him, an honour guard supplied by Heth. Just like politics, the cloak was an encumbrance that Daylight would dispense with in combat.

They moved up the quarterdeck, and under the valve-way arches. The burnished deck throbbed beneath them as the warship bled out power. The warp had just spat out the *Azimuth* after six and a half weeks of travel, and now, translated into the realm of real space, they and the rest of the reinforcement squadron were slicing in across the outer banks and belts of the Ardamantua System into the compliance zone.

As he walked, Daylight processed. Data-feeds were inflowing to his visor mount, and had been since the trip began. He processed the latest intercepts and battle reports from the line formation, archived data on the planet and the blisternest site, force composition and a rolling track of action-by-action detail from the very first moment of deployment onwards. From the outside, Daylight looked like a ceremonial figure walking in a grand state parade. On the inside, he was a strategium in war mode.

Most of the data he could process was archived, however. It came from the early part of the compliance, and from intercepts received before the reinforcement squadron had left the Terran Core. They had spent weeks in the empyrean, and nothing viable or reliable had entered the data-streams of astropathic communication links during the voyage.

Now they were back in real space, the vast leap of their extra-universal transit achieved, communication could resume.

Except, Daylight could see from the feeds, nothing was coming from the world called Ardamantua.

Nothing human.

He entered the warship's state bridge. Navy officers turned to acknowledge him with formal stiffness, but a gesture sent them back to their vast consoles, set in tiers up the mountainside flanks of the chamber. On high platforms with gilded handrails, strategy officers plotted courses and operated the vast hololithic displays of the central strategium. Lines of Navy armsmen in formal uniforms, in ranks forty long and seven wide, stood facing each other on the central, mirror-polished steel floorspace of the bridge, forming an avenue down which Daylight could proceed to the command dais. They came to attention, their silver lascarbines raised.

Daylight walked the line, still processing.

*Nothing human, nothing human...*

Admiral Kiran stepped off the dais to meet him, escorted by General Maskar and a small army of aides, subalterns and autoclerks. Kiran was Lansung's appointed proxy, a slender and unfriendly-looking man in late middle age with a permanently cunning expression on his face. He wore silver and blue, and a broad bicorn hat. He carried the ship's command wand in his left hand. The wand was a jewel-encrusted device the size of a sceptre or battle-mace, and it hummed soft songs of deep space and the warpways to itself.

Maskar was Lord Commander Militant Heth's proxy on the command warship, though Heth travelled with the squadron aboard the grand carrier *Dubrovnic*. Unlike Lansung, who had seen the Ardamantua crisis in purely political terms and had instructed his officers to conduct it on his behalf, Heth was a more selfless individual. He appreciated the potential scale of the crisis and had elected to join the reinforcements in person. He led sixty-eight brigades of the Astra Militarum, the biggest deployment from the core seen in years, and he was not about to place that in the hands of his juniors. Heth wanted to show that unlike Lansung and, indeed, the other High Lords, he was prepared to get his hands dirty. The Imperial Fists required the assistance of his Astra Militarum, and he intended to deliver that in person.

It had caused a stir when Heth had announced his intention of joining the squadron. There was nothing Lansung could say about it that wouldn't look petty, but Lansung's thunder had been stolen a little. Heth was positioning himself as a willing man of the people, a leader who *did* rather than *told*. It was clear that Heth saw this moment as an opportunity to show that the Astra Militarum, vast and reliable, was the most important service standing in the Imperium's defence, the truest and most doughty.

It was also an opportunity for Heth to ease himself out of the shadow cast across the Senatorium High Twelve by Lansung, Mesring and Udo.

As per protocol, not all the squadron's senior officers travelled on the same vessel. Vox-officers set up a real-time link to Heth so he could coordinate with them.

DAN ABNETT

Maskar was a useful officer, short and bullish, with an excellent track record. He had not long returned from service in a frontier campaign, the 'blood fresh on his tunic' as the phrase went. Daylight had read Maskar's file. He liked the man, liked him for what he could do.

None of that data was pertinent now: not Maskar's file, not the politics on Terra.

'Sir,' said Kiran.

'Anything?' asked Daylight. 'Anything from the surface?'

'No,' replied the admiral.

'Nothing human,' Maskar added with a growl.

'I have reviewed the incoming data,' said Daylight. 'It's very noisy down there.'

Kiran nodded to one of his analysis officers, who projected a small hololithic display between his tech-engraved hands as though he was opening a book for them to look at.

'Since our last data from Ardamantua,' the analysis officer said, 'the surface and atmospheric situations have degenerated catastrophically. The planet seems to have been plunged into some kind of stellar crisis. It's almost primordial down there. We presumed at first that it might have been struck by another body, a large meteor, but there is no trace of that very distinctive damage pattern.'

Daylight watched the man's shifting display, staying one step ahead of everything he said.

'Ardamantua has been rendered unstable in the six weeks since we last saw it,' the analysis officer continued. 'It is unstable atmospherically, geologically and orbitally. There are gross levels of surface radiation, and significant signs of massive gravitic instability.'

'There were never any indications of gravitic weaknesses in the early planetary surveys,' said Admiral Kiran.

'However,' said Maskar, 'some of the last few intercepts we received from the expedition force before we departed spoke of what appeared to be gravitational anomalies.'

'That data was never substantiated,' said the analysis officer. 'We have been attempting to contact Terra astropathically to see what they may have heard from the expedition fleet while we were in transit.'

'The answer is precious little, it seems,' said Kiran. He looked directly at the towering Space Marine. 'All effective contact with your Chapter Master and the expedition fleet was lost over six weeks ago, two days after we entered the warp.'

'So they are gone?' asked Daylight. 'Dead?'

'There is no sign of the fleet or of any surface deployment,' said Maskar. 'But that isn't to say they aren't there.'

'The planet and its orbital environs are a mess of interference patterns and disruption,' said the analysis officer. 'It is quite possible that the fleet is there, as well as surface forces, but our scanners can't detect them and we can't hear their vox.'

'So what are we hearing?' asked Daylight.

'Massive amounts of sonic and infrasonic noise bursts,' said the analysis officer, 'similar to the kind of noise bursts reported by the surface forces before comms went down, but of greater intensity, duration and regularity. It's as though the planet is howling in agony.'

Kiran shot the man a scolding look. The analysis officer stepped back, ashamed of his colourful description.

'What's making the noise?' asked Daylight.

'I think it's some kind of stellar effect,' said Kiran. 'A solar storm, perhaps, or a transmitted by-product of the gravitational mayhem.'

'Except,' said Maskar.

'Except?' asked Daylight.

'It reads as organic,' said Lord Commander Militant Heth's proxy. He said it hesitantly, as though he didn't quite believe it himself.

'How can it be organic?' asked Daylight.

'A voice,' murmured the analysis officer. 'It's like a voice...'

'It's something amplified and broadcast,' said Maskar.

'A weapon of some description?' suggested Kiran.

'What action do we take?' asked Maskar.

'We deploy, of course,' said the unmistakable tones of the Lord Commander Militant.

They turned. The vox and pict link had been established to the Lord Commander Militant's vessel, and his face, slightly crackled by interference patterns, had appeared in the ruddy field of a large hololithic projector unit.

'Is that not rash, my lord?' asked Admiral Kiran. 'We don't even know how close we can get and maintain the safety of the squadron.'

'We travelled six weeks to face a problem and perhaps save the lives of some honoured friends,' said Heth, his voice signal distorting slightly. 'We are also investigating a potential capital threat to the Terran Core. I don't think this is the time to be prissy. How long until we're inside a decent deployment distance, admiral?'

'Four hours and seventeen minutes,' replied Kiran.

'Are the men ready for planetary landing, general?' Heth asked.

'All infantry and armour support will be boarded on the drop-ships and surface landers within the hour, sir,' replied Maskar. 'I can commit a full force drop as soon as we are in range.'

'And the Imperial Fists?' asked Heth. 'The wall-brethren?'

'We are ready,' replied Daylight.

'Then the only thing that appears rash,' said Heth, 'is the notion of me making this decision rather than waiting to hear it from the nominated and honoured commander of this expedition. Forgive me, sir. The call is yours.'

There was a pause.

'Thank you, my lord,' said Daylight. 'Given the extremity of the conditions, I believe it would be prudent to arrange an advance recon, fast and powerful, to penetrate the zone and report back before we risk the bulk of our forces. I will lead this. Have a ship prepared.'

Daylight looked at Heth.

'The main force should be held at readiness. As soon as we have data, and as soon as an enemy or objective is identified, the fleet elements and the Imperial Guard will take it with the fury of the Emperor Himself. Does that seem like a plan to you, my lord?'

'I couldn't have put it better myself,' replied Heth.

'Then let us begin,' said Daylight.

'The Emperor protects,' nodded Maskar and Kiran, making the sign of the aquila.

'And we, in our turn,' replied Daylight, 'protect Him.'

# FIFTEEN

## Ardamantua

Like stooping raptors, pinions swept back for the long dive, the Stormbirds plunged into the swirling atmospheric halo surrounding stricken Ardamantua.

The planet was swathed by a bright, visible corona of agitated energy, a sensor-opaque aura that shrouded the orb to almost the depth of its own radius. It resembled a solar storm, a swirling, luminous ocean of gas, dust and radiation that flickered in blues, golds, ambers and reds. The planet itself was just a dark globe, silhouetted within the maelstrom.

Just as the wall-brothers had been drawn out of traditional service and allowed to roam away from Terra, so the Stormbird war machines, the fastest and most honoured of all the drop-craft in the arsenal of the Adeptus Astartes, had been selected for the reinforcement mission. Stormbirds, sleek, powerful and large-capacity, had been born in the earliest years of the Great Crusade, developed from the almost mythical Skylance drop-ships that had served during the final days of the Unification Wars splitting open the hives of Ceylonia and Ind. Stormbirds had been the inter-orbital weapon of choice throughout the Crusade, and through the dark, treacherous time that had been the unexpected sequel to that bright glory.

The Heresy had consumed them in great numbers, however, just as it had consumed men and brothers and Legions, and the forces of the Imperium had been obliged to resort to more utilitarian vehicles that were cheaper and easier to mass produce. These replacement craft were now ubiquitous in all Chapters, and had proved worthy of service through their simple functionality and durability.

Still, for those with long memories, there was nothing like a Stormbird to stir the heart. The symbol of the Emperor's wrath, wings hooked back like an aquila – one only saw them in ceremonial flypasts these days, or in the Hall of Weapons, or as escorts for High Lords, warmasters and sector governors.

Daylight had ordered six of them to be raised from the Fists' Chapter House hangars and stowed aboard the reinforcement fleet. No one had argued. Heth's presence on the campaign mission had helped. He was a High Lord, after all.

Firing from the capital ships like missiles, the Stormbirds formed a formation spread and scream-dived into the unholy vortex surrounding the planet. Ardamantua lay beneath them, a vast curve of grey mottled with orange and crackled with veins of fire. Cloud banks and storm patterns of vast magnitude curdled and swirled across the boiling surface. Magnetics, radiation and the pop of gravity blisters rendered the nearspace realm a lethal soup.

'We have substantial vulcanism around the equatorial belt,' reported the lead Stormbird's tech-adept. 'The crust there is faulting and splitting.'

The Stormbird was shaking. Daylight keyed up the data on his overhead monitor and swung it down on its gimbal arm. On the flickering pict, strung with overlays, the planet seemed to have a burning, white-hot girdle around its waist.

'Something's happening to the magnetic poles,' said the adept. 'The planet is deforming. I–'

His voice cut out briefly as another noise burst ripped through the vox-links, squalling and deafening. The screech was painful, but Daylight's ears could endure it. He had a concern for the human component of his task-force, however. The unmodified, unaugmented humans of the Imperial Guard formed the greatest proportion of his strikeforce. They would suffer, either through mortal injury from the noise bursts, or through lack of coordination if vox-comm proved unviable. What were the implications if he was unable to deploy any of his Guard strength to the surface? Could the wall-brothers complete the mission unassisted? Could they find and rescue the shield-corps?

*Rescue* was a word he certainly did not like.

The Stormbird began to shake more furiously as they entered the outer radiation bands of the high atmosphere. Plumes of what looked like flame flashed past the small, semi-shuttered cabin ports. The tongues were blue, mauve and green, like noxious gases burning in a lab. For a moment, Daylight wondered if they were some trace of the warp, some daemonic lightning. All along there had been quiet rumours that the silent hand of Chaos, whose actions had been absent from the galactic theatre for a troublingly long time, might be playing a part in the Arda-mantuan misadventure.

But it was not false fire or warp-scald. It was a geomagnetic display, auroras of charged particles ripping through the maddened thermosphere.

'Any indication of vessels in nearspace?' asked Daylight.

'Negative,' replied the tech-adept.

Another hope dashed. There was a fleet here, somewhere, the best part of the entire Imperial Fists battlefleet, unless it had been utterly reduced and annihilated already. Where was it? It could be directly in front of them, but veiled from them by the tumult.

The descent turbulence became progressively worse. The Stormbird was shaking like a sistrum at a fervent ritual. Lines of red alert lights were flashing into life along the pilot's enclosing consoles, filling entire rows. Deftly, with great calm, the pilot took one black-leather-gloved hand off the helm and muted the alarms.

Daylight began to flick through the meagre and imperfect surface scan readings they were finally obtaining, as they got closer and their auspex systems penetrated the atmosphere a little more deeply. They were on a pre-selected dive towards the location of the blisternest, working on the tactical assumption that the site was the last place their forces had been reported. But there was no clear sign of the structure, and little of the surrounding landmass matched, in relief or topographical schemata form at least, the geography logged by the survey teams that had accompanied the original assault.

'Is this just bad luck?' asked Zarathustra.

Daylight turned and looked at the wall-brother strapped in beside him. Zarathustra's war-spear was mounted like a harpoon on the weapon rack above his grim-helmed head. He was the oldest of all the wall-brothers and had been the most reluctant to abandon the old tradition and leave the walls of the Palace behind.

'Bad luck?' replied Daylight. He noted that Zarathustra had selected the discretion of a helm-to-helm link. There were other wall-brothers in the craft alongside them, not to mention forty atmospherically-armoured shock troops of the Astra Militarum Asmodai Seventieth, Heth's finest. The Guardsmen and their leader, Major Nyman, seemed to Daylight to be about the finest and most resolute warriors that unmodified human flesh could compose, but he did not want them overhearing dissent from an Adeptus Astartes warrior as they fell headlong into Hades. Through the dark and slightly breath-fogged visor lenses of their faceplates, he could see pale, drawn, anxious faces that winced at every violent buck and lurch the Stormbird threw.

'Bad luck happens even to good men, Daylight,' said Zarathustra, his voice chopped and frayed by the interference patterns even on the short-range dedicated link. 'Sometimes the forces of light prevail, sometimes the forces of darkness take the upper hand. Sometimes, as history teaches us, fate itself intervenes.'

He turned his impassive visor to look directly at Daylight. There was a gouge of raw metal across the otherwise perfectly polished faceplate, a gouge that had been left by the blade of one of the Sons of Horus during the fight at Zarathustra Wall. Heresy wounds were never patched, though the brother who had taken that stroke no longer dwelt inside the armour.

'Think of Coldblood and his wall, at Orphan Mons,' said Zarathustra. 'They took that day against the eldar raiders, full of glory. Then the star went nova and took Coldblood, his wall and the surviving eldar. Victor and defeated alike, levelled by the whim of the conscienceless cosmos.'

'They say the eldar corsairs engineered that stellar bomb to effect a pyrrhic victory,' said Daylight.

'They say... they say... Don't spoil my story,' grumbled Zarathustra. 'My point is sound. Sometimes you kill the enemy, sometimes the enemy kills you, and sometimes the universe kills you both. This may have been a very conventional fight against these xenoforms, these Chrome things. Mirhen was probably wiping the floor with them, soaking the dust with their blood, or whatever they have that passes for blood...'

Zarathustra's eye-slits were milky pale, and back-lit by a faint green glow, but Daylight could feel the intensity of his old friend's gaze upon him.

'Then the planet dies. Solar storm. Gravity anomaly. Tachyon event. Whatever. Doesn't matter who's winning then. We end up with a mess like this.'

Daylight glanced at his overhead again. The only time he had ever seen data footage of a planet as catastrophically mangled and tortured as Ardamantua was in feeds of unstable worlds to be avoided as 'not supportive'. Six weeks earlier, the cream of his Chapter, the majority of his kin, the shield-corps itself, had been down there, dug in and on a solid footing, burning out the last vestiges of a numerous but outclassed enemy.

'Are you suggesting we turn back and give them up as lost?' he asked.

'Of course not.'

'Then what?'

'I'm suggesting that we prepare ourselves for the worst,' said Zarathustra. 'If this mudball has up and died under Master Mirhen and our brothers, then...'

'We will make a great mourning like never before, greater even than we did for our Primarch-Progenitor,' said Daylight, simply.

'It would be the worst loss imaginable,' agreed Zarathustra. 'For the Imperial Fists, the Old Seventh, greatest of all the Adeptus Astartes, and the most loyal of all defenders of Terra, to be reduced to... to nothing, to nothing but the last fifty wall-brothers stationed at the Palace. To lose all but five per cent, to be diminished to a twentieth... How would we ever recover from that?'

Daylight had no answer. Zarathustra was right. It was unthinkable. Even a force of transhuman warriors dedicated to dying in the service of the Imperium did not like to consider what might happen if they *all* died. The gene-seed loss alone would be an atrocity. Could they ever rebuild, even turning to Successor Chapters for support and bloodline? No loyal First Founding Chapter had ever been entirely swept away, not in the history of the Imperium, not even in the Heresy War.

Would the Imperial Fists be the first to pass into legend?

Some said, quietly and very informally, that it was

inevitable. The Adeptus Astartes were a dying breed. Blood-lines and gene-seeds were gradually failing over time. The vigour had waned, and long gone was the time, pre-Heresy, when thousands upon thousands of Space Marines marshalled under the stars. The bitter gall of the Heresy had cut them down, halved their Legions, decimated the surviving loyalists, and tragically reduced the Chapters' ability to produce new Space Marines in anything like the numbers of old. With the possible exception of the Ultramarines – and even there, there was the contention that the same plight ultimately afflicted them too – the Adeptus Astartes were diminishing. They were a finite resource, used only for the most elite missions and efforts. They were slowly, very slowly, dying out. Senior men in the Chapter predicted that within four or five hundred years, unless effective new methods of gene-seed synthesis could be developed and a new Golden Age brought about, the Space Marine would be a thing of myth.

In his early life, before the honour of wall-brother had been granted him, before he had become Daylight, Day-light had fought the eldar. In fact, it was his deeds in the face of the eldar that had led to the wall-brother honour being bestowed upon him.

Daylight had admired the eldar immensely. They were truly worthy opponents, and he had always thought them sad, tragic, like figures in an ancient play. He had thought about them often as he paced the ritual patrol routes in the cold hallways of Daylight Wall. They were great warriors, the greatest their species could produce, and in their time, in older ages, they had been peerless among the infinite stars.

Their time had passed, however, and their glory with it. Their suns were setting, and they were but ghosts of their old selves, unimpeachable warriors with great stories, proud histories, old glories and fine hearts, who were simply fighting their end-day wars as they waited for extinction to overwhelm them. When Daylight had slain the crest-helmed master of Sethoywan Craftworld, there had been tears in the alien's eyes, and tears in Daylight's too. When great eras end, all should mark them, even the champions of the next epoch. And no great heroes should ever pass unto shadow unmourned.

For a long time, Daylight had felt that the Space Marines were facing a similar long decline. They were more like the worthy eldar than they cared to admit: giants from another age who were simply living out their twilight amongst mortals, incapable of fending off the gathering darkness, and unable to recapture their halcyon greatness.

Daylight had not expected to see that end approach so fast inside his own lifespan. If the Imperial Fists were as lost as Zarathustra feared, perhaps the age of the Adeptus Astartes was coming to a close faster than anyone imagined.

Zarathustra's words had troubled him in another way. He had spoken of the terrain turning against friend and foe alike, of Ardamantua and its geological mayhem being the true enemy.

That was a bleak prospect. The pride of the Imperial Fists was their ability to defend anywhere from anything. How could they hope to excel if anywhere and everywhere, the very ground itself turned on them?

The Stormbird bucked again, more violently than ever.

More warning lights lit and a klaxon sounded. The pilot and his co-pilot were too busy controlling the breakneck descent to be able to cancel it this time. The lurching turned into a protracted bout of shuddering vibrations.

'Atmospherics worse than cogitator prediction,' said the tech-adept, a flutter in his tone. 'Crosswinds... also, ash in the upper airbands.'

'Ash?'

'Volcanic ash, also particulate matter. Aerosolised mud. Organic residue.'

'Hold on!' the pilot yelled suddenly.

The Stormbird started to bank along its centre line. The exterior light beaming into the gloom of the cabin through the slit ports began to rapidly creep up the cabin walls, over the ceiling and back down the other side, illuminating the struggling, desperate faces of the Asmodai troopers behind their visor plates, cheeks and chins tugged by the inverting gravity.

The banking turned into a full rotation, then another, and then another, faster. Daylight knew that the humans aboard weren't built to withstand that kind of flight trauma. The Stormbird crew members were modified enough to withstand it, with their reinforced bones and muscle sheaths, their inner ears and proprioception senses replaced by augmetics, and their stomachs and regurgitative mechanisms removed and regrafted with fluid ingesters. But the Imperial Guardsmen would be disorientated, panicked, distressed, vomiting inside their helmets, choking.

'Stabilise!' Daylight ordered.

'Negative! Negative!' the pilot yelled back. 'We've hit some kind of gravitational–'

He didn't finish the word. The turbulence became too great and too noisy for voice contact. The unpredictable gravitational anomalies that plagued Ardamantua were regarded as the greatest threat of all because they couldn't be mapped and thus avoided.

And they couldn't be explained.

Daylight heard the pilot yell something again.

On the ground, a broad plain of mud and boiling pools lay beneath the angry sky. Ragged grasses blew in the hot crosswinds. In the distance, the broken horizon coughed and smoked, and spat sparks into the sky.

The sky was low, a rotting mass of swirling cloud striped by lightning. The clouds were running swiftly across it, like a pict-feed playing fast. Far away, six bright raptors punched out of the clouds, diving, catching the sun. They stayed in formation for a second, but they were fluttering, beset by both savage crosswinds and a gravitational pocket that refused to obey the reality around it.

One burst into flames, like a flower blooming, scattering its shredded fuselage. A second failed to recover from its dive, and plunged like a stone into the distant hills. A third tried to bank, but then spun away like a leaf on the wind, out of sight.

The other three stayed true, pulled up, cut low, but their trajectories were not stable either.

Gravity stammered again, bubbling the sky and slamming them hard.

They fell into darkness and black cloud, and were lost.

# SIXTEEN

## Ardamantua

Anterior Six was dead. They carried him from the crash site and laid him next to the nine Asmodai fatalities. Daylight waited for Nyman to tell him the extent of the other injuries.

Zarathustra clambered back into the wreck to recover his spear. Daylight knew he was also going to mercifully finish off the valiant pilot and co-pilot who had brought them down as intact as they were, and now lay mashed and bleeding out in the Stormbird's compressed nosecone. They were plugged into the drop-craft's systems anyway, nerves and neural links. They had burned their minds out sharing the Stormbird's impact agonies. Even without their limbs and torsos irrecoverably sandwiched in ruptured metal, they could never have been disconnected to walk away.

It was a duty Daylight would have preferred to do, but he had command, and there were too many duties to deal with. He appreciated Zarathustra taking that sad burden from him.

He looked down at Anterior Six's body. On impact, a fracturing spar had sheared the wall-brother's head off.

'I never thought I'd see him dead,' said Tranquility, at Daylight's side.

The plain they had come down on was a broad one surrounded by low, smoke-dark hills. It was grassy, and peppered with curiously pretty blue flowers. Some of the petals, torn up by the crash and scattered by the wind, had fallen across Anterior Six's yellow armour, as if laid there by mourners.

'No time for sentiment,' said Daylight. 'Give me a situation report, brother.'

Tranquility cleared his throat.

'Flight crew dead, Daylight,' he said. 'Transport destroyed, vox-link down. No bearing from our instrumentation and portable auspex is flatlined. Last known location was forty kilometres short of the blisternest site.'

Daylight nodded.

'No contact with the other birds,' said Tranquility.

'I saw one blow out.'

'I think at least one other crashed before we hit,' Tranquility agreed. 'Gravity was just shot. We probably all fell out of the sky.'

'So we're all that we can count on,' said Daylight.

'There might be others nearby who survived the landing and–' Tranquility began.

'This is not a place where we can deal in "mights",' replied Daylight. 'Even the laws of the universe are playing tricks. We can only count on what we know.'

'I understand,' replied Tranquility. 'Then we have you, and we have me. We have Zarathustra and we have Bastion Ledge. We have decent resources of ammunition and our close-combat weapons. We have no ground transport. We have Major Nyman, a brain-damaged tech-adept, and twenty-six Imperial Guardsmen with kit.'

'I thought there were nine fatalities amongst the Asmodai?'

'There were, outright. But there are another five more of them are too torn up to walk away. Out here, they'll all be dead in an hour, less perhaps. Even with express evacuation to a medicae frigate, they probably wouldn't make it.'

'We move out,' said Daylight. 'Find high vantage. Assess the landscape and consider our next action.'

Tranquility nodded.

Daylight strode back through the flowering grasses towards the Stormbird wreck. Zarathustra was just emerging, spear in hand. He reminded Daylight of one of the ancient, pre-Unity demigods, born alive from the belly of a fallen eagle. He liked the old myths. Paintings and tapestries of them filled the galleries and halls of the Imperial Palace, their meanings, names and symbolism lost forever, except perhaps in the memories and dreams of the Emperor.

'Bad?' asked Zarathustra.

'And getting worse,' Daylight replied. 'We're heading for those hills. You and I will move ahead with Bastion. Tranquility can escort the Guardsmen.'

'We should stay together.'

'They'll slow us down. They'll never cover the ground like we can. Besides, they're in shock.'

'What of their wounded? They'll make them even slower.'

'I know. I'll do it.'

They walked back to the gathered survivors. A few of the Asmodai were carrying munitions and equipment crates from the opened stowage cavities of the Stormbird. Others crouched beside their injured brethren. Daylight noted that a few had formed a perimeter, lasweapons ready. Not in *such* shock, then. They remembered their duty.

The sun came out suddenly, covering the ragged plain and its sea of straw-coloured grasses and nodding flowers in a hot golden light. The roiling black clouds had parted briefly. The Stormbird had torn a two-kilometre scar across the ground, a long gouge like the one that the Horusian blade had left on Zarathustra's faceplate. The Stormbird's impact had ripped up grasses and soil and bedrock, and scattered silvered shreds of its bodywork, wings and undercarriage. The fragments of metal caught the sudden sunlight like pieces of mirror or broken glass scattered in the swishing grasses, or like the cut jewels of a broad cloak spread out behind the noble craft.

'We're moving for those hills,' Daylight told Major Nyman.

'I've activated a beacon, sir,' said Nyman. His voice was a reedy croak issuing through the speaker grille of his orbital armour. Through the tint of the man's visor, Daylight could see an abrasion head wound that was starting to clot.

'Good. At least any who follow can trace our landing point.'

'Will any follow?' asked Nyman.

Daylight was turning away, but he stopped to look back down at the human soldier.

'I told them not to, but Lord Commander Militant Heth will send others,' he said. 'He will not give up. I would not in his place.'

Nyman followed Daylight over to the Asmodai casualties.

'Some of us will scout ahead,' Daylight told him, 'but even

allowing for your rate of advance, we cannot be encumbered. You know what I have to do.'

Nyman's mouth opened in horror, but he had no words.

'They will all be dead in an hour, less perhaps,' put in Tranquility, repeating the summation he'd made to Daylight. 'Even with express evacuation to a medicae frigate, they probably wouldn't make it.'

There was a moment's pause. The sunlight blazed. Radiation made their built-in meters crackle like crickets at dusk. Thunder, wind and volcanics rumbled in the distance and made the ground fidget.

'Is there going to be an issue here?' Daylight asked Major Nyman.

'No issue, sir,' Nyman replied with great effort. He turned his back, and signalled his men to do the same. In slow realisation and horror, they stepped back and looked towards the bleak edges of the horizon bowl. One hesitated, a hand on the grip of his sidearm. Bastion looked at him, and that was enough.

Zarathustra came to stand with Nyman and his men, and gazed at the distant hills and the sky filled with smoke. He began to declare the Litany of the Fallen, as it was said in chapels and templums and sacristies across the loving Imperium, the words set down by Malcador himself during the bloodiest months of the Heresy. His voice was clear and strong, and carried from the speaker of his battle-helm. Bastion and Tranquility joined him in his declaration, a mark of honour to the fallen Guard and the sacrifice of the Asmodai. Nyman made the sign of the aquila.

The three wall-brothers boosted the amplification of their

speakers as they intoned the Litany, partly to add power to their statement of respect, and partly to mask the sound of bones snapping.

Daylight drew a breath and then, quickly and gently, broke five human necks in quick succession.

# SEVENTEEN

## Ardamantua

The sunlight seemed to be at odds with them. It followed them across the grassy plain, away from the crash site. From underfoot came the thump and shake of a planet in convulsion, and great sprays of burning ash lit up the sky far away, volcanic plumes thousands of kilometres wide.

The sunlight followed them still, as if their world were a tranquil place.

Daylight, Zarathustra and Bastion moved ahead, covering the grasses with clean, strong, bounding strides, outpacing the sturdy efforts of Nyman's fighting pack. Daylight wondered if he ought to have finished the tech-adept too. The man had been cortex-plugged to the Stormbird's cogitator system when they crashed. He had suffered neural feedback, and the impact had torn his plug out and mangled the primary socket in the back of his neck. He was stumbling along at the back of the secondary group, escorted by one of the Guardsmen. Daylight thought he would give him an hour or so to see if his head cleared and reset. If it did, the adept might usefully operate some of their portable equipment. If it didn't, Daylight would revise his decision.

Plumes of ash smoke and white streamers of steam were borne across the plain on the wind, residue of distant cataclysms. They left the crash site far behind, the wreck and the heresy-scar of its death across a foreign field, and moved towards the nearest hills.

Noise bursts continued to beset them, coming from both near at hand and far away, as if wilderness spirits, the genius loci of Ardamantua, were howling at them and taunting them for their efforts. Daylight wished the tech-adept could set up and examine the audio patterns, but the man was incapable. The noise bursts, some of them long and tortured, were overwhelming their limited-range vox too, and causing discomfort to the Asmodai. Daylight instructed Nyman and his men to switch off their suit comms. Thus, the only communication between the two moving groups was the vox-link between Daylight's party and Tranquility who was escorting the Guard. It was not ideal.

Daylight also possessed enough imagination to know that it was not ideal for the individual Guardsmen either. Each one of them was alone in his stifling and cumbersome orbital drop-suit, the armour heavy and rubbing, with fear and disorientation in his heart, and trauma and grief in his bones. They were trudging along in the strange and sickly sunlight, hearing the distant roar of the noise bursts as contact vibrations transmitted by their atmospheric armour-helms, with no voices and no vox-chatter, only the inexorable sound of their own breathing inside their suits for company.

The three Space Marines, advancing away from the belea-
guered troopers, were approaching the foothill slopes of
the ragged outcrops that edged the plain. Now the sun was
going in and out as clouds gathered and spilled across the
sky. Something had detonated on the horizon and the sky
was filling up with blackness, the smoke trying to erase
every corner of light.

Zarathustra led the way, using the haft of his war-spear as
a climbing staff, leaping up slumped boulders and ridges
of displaced stone. Bastion and Daylight followed, almost
amused by the old veteran's vitality.

They reached the peak. Beyond them, a thousand kilometres away, the next ridge of mountains was on fire, a ring
of active volcanos. Darkness seemed to have gathered above
the next rift valley like a threat. Jagged and almost magical
explosions rippled across the valley floor as spontaneous
and random gravitational anomalies, like the one that had
downed the Stormbirds, chewed up the ground and blew
sub-crust magma into the air. Impact patterns of disruption on a seismic level travelled through the ground away
from the explosions. At this sight, Daylight's mind turned
to other images stored in the books and paintings of the
Imperial Palace: visions of the apocalypse, of the circles of
the Inferno described by Dantey, of the imagined hell once
thought to exist beneath the Earth.

The rift valley was a vast plain of smouldering rubble
that shifted and flexed, exploded and shivered. Mountains
had both been raised and had fallen, overnight. Valleys
had uplifted into hills, fracturing the surface, and sum-
mits had plunged like avalanches into the bowels of the

ground. Flames leapt up from the mangled earth in burning geysers, like signs or portents. Flammable noxious gases released from deep in the planet were burning with strange colours: purple, blue, green, yellow, as varied as the magnetic auroras that had wreathed their wings on their descent.

In places, the flames were black, and a mile high.

'Has the Archenemy touched this place?' asked Bastion Ledge cautiously. 'Is that warpcraft?'

'No,' said Daylight. 'This is just a planet dying. Strange phenomena manifest when a planet dies.'

Four or five kilometres from them, beyond the initial spill of rubble and rocks, there was a broad lake, silty and muddy, its surface stirred and chopped by wind and vibration. Daylight selected data from his helm memory and began to patch and re-patch quick overlays.

'That's the river,' he said.

'The river?' asked Bastion Ledge.

'The blisternest was sited beside a large river. The geography has been traumatically altered, but that is the river, I'm sure of it. There are just enough comparatives to make the connection. The river has broken its banks and over-spilled, and then been dammed into the lake formation by the collapsing outcrops *here* and *here*. The blisternest will be partly submerged and, I think, partly covered by geological debris, but it should be in this position.'

He marked the proposed site on his optics and then copy-bursted the overlay to the visor displays of his two wall-brothers.

'An objective, then?' asked Bastion Ledge.

'The blisternest was the last reported location of our shield-corps ground forces,' said Daylight.

'Ardamantua was the last reported location,' growled Zarathustra. 'I don't think we can say anything more specific than that.'

'We'll head for it anyway,' said Daylight. 'It's a place to start.'

He clambered back across the ragged top of the peak to vox-link to Tranquility and inform the secondary group what the new intention was.

Below, he saw the flash of lasweapons discharging. In the sunlit grassland, under an alien storm of ash, Tranquility and Nyman's Asmodai Guardsmen were under attack.

# EIGHTEEN

## Ardamantua

It was a Chrome. Major Nyman knew this because he'd thoroughly reviewed the briefing packet that had been circulated among the officers of the reinforcement taskforce, and the packet had included helm pict-captures of the Chromes in action.

It came at him through the grass, claws raised and mouth-parts snapping, making a most peculiar noise that he could only half-hear in the claustrophobic isolation of his atmospheric armour.

He shouted an order that he instantly realised no one except him could actually hear, brought his laspistol up and shot two bolts at the charging xenos.

It slowed it down, but didn't kill it. Nyman had to snap off four more shots before it dropped a few metres short of where he was standing.

He looked around, having to turn his whole body to maximise the view through his narrow visor port. He could hear his own rapid respiration, as if he was in a box. He could smell the rancid bitterness of his sweat and breath, laced with adrenaline. Muffled noises came to him, as though through water. The dull bangs of weapons. Shouts. Sunlight shone into his visor. Glare.

There were Chromes all around them, most of them the glossy silver xenotype. He wasn't sure where they had come from, but the odds were they were burrowers and had come up through the soil, clawing their way out. His men, without orders to give them structure, had nevertheless obeyed essential combat drill and were forming a box, firing out at the things rushing them from all sides. The Asmodai were fine soldiers, trained by the very best in the gun schools of the old Panpacific. Their proud boast to be the best in the Astra Militarum was not without merit.

Lasrifles flashed and snapped in disciplined volleys, the searing las-bolts ripping open organic armour and mutilating limbs. Puffs and squirts of ichor drizzled into the bright air.

One of the Chromes, a very large, dark variant form, survived the rifle-fire barrage and made it to their line. It got Corporal Vladen in its claws and tore him in half, the way a man would rip a sheet of paper when he was done reading the message written on it. Ribbons of bright red blood shivered into the air and covered the grass. Vladen's armoured suborbital drop-suit split like overheated plastek wrapping.

Tranquility, the massive Imperial Fist, waded in, and drove the dark creature back, striking it twice with his power hammer. Leaking fluids through crush-splits in its shell, the Chrome reared back and launched itself at the Space

Marine. There was no time or space for a defensive swing. Tranquility met the heavily built animal and grappled with it, gripping its chattering mouthparts with his left hand and tearing, while he tried to stave off its claws. As they broke again, Tranquility came away with part of a mandible in his hand. Ichor spurted down the Chrome's throat and chest. Tranquility knocked it down with a hammerblow and then swung his power hammer down in both hands and finished it with a devastating overhead strike.

More Chromes tore up out of the ground, flinging soil and uprooted grasses in all directions. Some of them were big and dark like the thing that had murdered Vladen. The Asmodai redoubled their fire rate, snapping off shots to keep the creatures at maximum distance. Nyman kept shooting, directing fire by means of gestures.

There was no way of knowing how many more of the things lay under the ground.

Tranquility closed with another of the more massive forms, despatched it with two clean blows of his hammer, and then found himself beset by two more of the dark beasts. They clawed at him, fending off his attempts to swing at them. With a curse, he drew his boltgun and shot each one point-blank, exploding their carcasses in showers of meat, gristle and body fluid.

He'd cut them a path. Nyman could see that, and he could plainly see the Space Marine's emphatic gestures. They had a path towards the hill slopes. In the distance, he could see the other Imperial Fists wall-brothers bounding down the hill to join them.

The hill slopes offered the protection of boulders and

rocks for cover, and a small hope of staying alive until the other Space Marines reached them. Nyman knew his men would have to double time, and shoot as they ran.

He sent the signal, and most of them started to move, but visibility in the suits was so poor that some missed the gesture and found themselves caught out, alone. Nyman ran to them, grabbing them so he could look in through their visor plates and press his head against theirs, yelling so that the touching helms would transmit the sound.

'Get moving! The hills! Move it, man!'

They started running. Nyman and Trooper Fernis scurried the poor tech-adept along. The damaged man had little clue what was going on. Trooper Galvet had been slow to recognise the intended effort, and once he did, ran the wrong way. Nyman, dismayed, believed that Galvet had suffered some concussion during the crash, and was not thinking clearly.

His fuzziness cost him his life. Two silver-shelled Chromes ran him down and fell upon him, shredding him with their claws.

Nyman didn't watch. He ran, dragging the tech-adept by the arm with one hand, firing at the Chromes that menaced them with his weapon in the other.

As soon as the Asmodai were moving towards the hill slopes, Tranquility fell in behind them, his back to them, retreating and fending off the Chromes that gave chase. He whirled his hammer and struck them down as they came at him, knocking them over onto their backs, splitting their shells, breaking their limbs and their spines. His power hammer was a long-hafted, weaponised version of a stonemason's mallet, the sort of tool that had been used to raise the bulwark walls and defences of the Palace of Terra. Its design was symbolic. Its effect was not.

Nyman, still moving with Trooper Fernis and their befuddled charge, was suddenly aware of yellow shapes racing past them from the direction of the slope. Daylight, Bastion Ledge and Zarathustra had joined the fight.

Daylight had his gladius raised. Zarathustra was lifting his war-spear. Bastion Ledge hefted a power mace. They reached the line where Tranquility was single-handedly stopping the Chromes and crashed into the mass of them, rending and slicing, smashing and tearing.

Nyman reached the lowest of the heaped boulders at the foot of the slope, and pushed the tech-adept into cover, with a gesture to Fernis to look after him. His men were taking up positions among the tufted rocks and outcrops, slithering up the scree and loose pebbles and sighting their rifles as they found good firing places.

They looked back at the fight.

Several hundred Chromes, most of them silver-shelled, had broken out of the soil of the plain and were assaulting the line. Dozens of them already lay dead, generally split or sliced open. Steam from hot fluids clouded the cool air of the grassy plain. Overhead, a looming volcanic darkness threatened to close down the light.

The four Imperial Fists, wall-brothers, battle-kin, shield-corps, fought side by side. It was diligent work, dutiful work, holding ground so that the Guardsmen could find cover and in turn support them with directed fire. It was a blocking action, it was a defensive stance, it was *holding ground*, it was everything that the Imperial Fists did best.

Daylight knew that none of them, none of the four of them, would or could ever admit that joy was filling them at that moment. Despite the crisis, the predicament, the threat, and the possibility that their Chapter was lost and dead, they secretly felt joy.

Their greatest and darkest prayer to the God-Emperor of Mankind, and to the Primarch-Progenitor who sired them, had been answered.

After years of silence, ritually patrolling the walls of the Imperial Palace, they had been granted the right to fight again, perhaps for one last time.

War, for which they had been wrought, had finally admitted them back into its secret, dark and savage mystery. They were whole again. They would make the most of it.

Nyman and his men watched in awe as the four wall-brothers fought back the tide. Imperial Fists chosen as wall-brothers were the greatest of their kind, and had excelled at feats of arms. It was for their very excellence that they were selected as the embodiment of the Chapter's creed, and set to stand guard on the walls where they had mounted their greatest defence and paid in blood.

He could see why these men had been chosen.

He could also see how many more Chromes, hulking and dark-bodied, were splitting the soil of the plain and clawing their way into the sunlight.

# NINETEEN

## Ardamantua – orbital

'Any signal from the surface?' asked Admiral Kiran.

The vox-officer shook his head.

Kiran slowly crossed the bridge of the *Azimuth* to meet Maskar and Lord Commander Militant Heth. Heth had joined them from his warship as the reinforcement fleet decelerated to the drop-point.

'We've lost them, then,' said Maskar. 'Sheer madness going down into that murk and mayhem blind.'

Heth looked at him.

'I suggest you get your men ready, Maskar, because you'll be following soon enough. We're not going to leave the Imperial Fists to rot down there.'

'And what makes you suspect they are anything except dead already, sir?' asked Maskar. 'With respect, look at the screens. Look at the dataflow. This is a fool's errand. Nothing has survived the fate that has befallen Ardamantua. Not even their damned fleet survived.'

'We give them another five hours,' said Heth. 'That's my

word on it. Five hours, then we send in more scouts. The first thing Daylight will do is set up a workable uplink or send some kind of signal.'

Maskar looked at Kiran. There was no love lost between the Navy man and the Guard commander, but they were thinking the same thing. Heth, a High Lord, was painfully out of touch. He clearly thought the Adeptus Astartes immortal. There were certain situations, certain conditions, certain environments, that nothing could survive. They were both working men, fighting men, and they had seen how bad it could actually get, not how bad it could be imagined from a throne in the Palace.

'Move the picket ships in closer,' Admiral Kiran told his deck officers. 'Have them despatch more long-range probes.'

'Probes will be obliterated, just like the last spread,' said Maskar.

'Some may survive,' replied Kiran curtly. 'Even if one of them survives to send back a millisecond of data, it will help. Besides, with the picket ships closer to the atmospheric rim, we can try penetrating deeper with auspex and primary sensors.'

Heth nodded. The deck officers hurried to their stations and began to relay instructions.

They watched the strategium display as the reinforcement fleet began to move into its new spread, circling the stricken planet. Indicator lights and icons drifted like sunlight dapples across the topographic grid. In the lower portion of the strategium's vast hololithic array, columns of data spread, jumbled and reassembled, processing the energetic flux and signature of the planet. Kiran had never

seen a planetary body generate so much wild and contra-
dictory data so rapidly.

'Wait!' he said, suddenly.

He crossed to one of the observation consoles and shoved
two sensor-adepts out of his way. He began to manipulate
the controls himself.

'What are you doing?' asked Heth.

Kiran didn't reply immediately. Most of the crew in
the huge bridge space were watching him. Kiran irritably
yanked off his gloves so he could better manipulate the
control surfaces. His fingers wound back the brass dials
and adjusted the ivory sliders until he had recaptured the
data-stream information from a few moments before.

'There,' he said.

'I don't know what I'm supposed to be looking at,' Maskar
ventured.

'Admiral, please elucidate,' said Heth.

'I know what I'm seeing,' said Kiran, 'and I'm sure my
senior officers do too.' In truth, many of them hadn't immediately recognised it. Few had Kiran's years of experience,
and few had seen as much cosmological data speed by
them as the admiral had, but given a few seconds, with the
data-stream artificially suspended and frozen, they could
pick it up.

'A ghost,' said the primary auspex supervisor.

'A ghost,' agreed Kiran with a grin.

'It could just be an imaging artifact,' said the gunnery
officer.

'Or the echo of a piece of debris blown out by the surface disruption?' suggested the oldest of the navigation

adepts, running the same data through his own, handheld quantifier.

'I don't believe it is,' said Kiran. 'I think that's a ghost, the ghost of a friend.'

Heth and Maskar moved closer to the vast display, trying to work out what everyone seemed to be seeing.

'This blip?' asked the Lord Commander Militant. 'This shadow here against the relative lower hemisphere of the planet?'

'Yes, my lord,' said Kiran. 'Sensorus! Have the advancing picket ships direct their full-gain auspex and detector grids at that shadow. And the fleet too, for what it's worth. Address all our scanning arrays, passive and active, at what the Lord Commander calls "that blip" and have the data streamed to my console.'

'But what is it?' asked Maskar.

'It's a ship, my dear general,' said Kiran. 'One of ours.'

# TWENTY

## Ardamantua – orbital

The ship emerged from the elemental fury surrounding Ardamantua, rising out of the radioactive soup and lashing ocean of charged particles like a wreck brought up from the seabed. Streams of energy and magnetic backwash, lurid and phosphorescent, spilled back into the pulsing blister of gravitational madness encasing the planet.

The ship rose, powered by its own half-failing engines, summoned by the frantic hails from Kiran's ships, voices that gave it a direction to head in. It was ailing and damaged, they could see that. Many decks were blown out and the hull was ruptured as though titanic battles had been waged on every level. At least one of its main engines was dead and bleeding clouds of lethal atomic blood into the vacuum.

Two of Kiran's most powerful cruisers, at the admiral's direction, moved in closer to the struggling revenant and secured tractor beams, slowly hauling back and assisting its desperate ascent from the cauldron of seething cosmological destruction.

DAN ABNETT

'Identity?' asked Lord Commander Militant Heth.

'It's Aggressor-class, my lord,' said Kiran, 'which means it has to be either the *Amkulon* or the *Ambraxas*. They were the two Aggressor-class cruisers assigned to the Chapter Master's undertaking.'

'Keel number and auto-broadcast codes confirm it is the *Amkulon*, sir,' a sensory officer announced.

'Let's raise her now she's clear of the backwash,' said Kiran. He walked over to the main communication station, where plugged-in operators and servitors worked at the steep banks of titanium keys. They looked as though they were attempting to play some nightmarishly complex cathedral pipe organ, out of which only the clacks and taps of their keys would issue.

'Connect me,' said Kiran.

Eerie squeals and screams suddenly blew up out of the vox-speakers, the ambient sound of space being tortured by radiation and gravity. Beeping and pulsing signals resolved out of the screams. Hololithic energies crackled around the cable-fed and rack-mounted hoop of the station's projector array, and then an image began to shimmer into place, suspended inside the rim of the hoop like soapy water inside a child's bubble-blower.

There was a great deal of distortion. They could see a face, but it seemed like a face as seen through a white veil of mourning, or some cerecloth for funereal binding.

'This is Admiral Kiran, commanding the reinforcement squadron. I am speaking from the bridge of my vessel, the *Azimuth*. *Amkulon*, can you hear me?'

Static. The moaning of vacuum ghosts.

'*Amkulon, Amkulon*, this is *Azimuth*. Can you hear me?'

'It is my pleasure to confirm that I can, admiral,' a broken voice said from the projector and the speakers. 'We thought we were lost. Lost forever. This is *Amkulon*. This is *Amkulon*. Shipmistress Aquilinia speaking.'

'Aquilinia! By the Throne, it's good to hear your voice,' said Kiran.

'Have you come to save us all, admiral? That will be quite a feat. The brave fleet is gone. Ardamantua is dying and it is taking the last of our best along with it.'

'Shipmistress,' Heth said, stepping up beside Kiran. 'Forgive me, this is Lord Commander Militant Heth. I am commanding this taskforce that has come to reinforce and assist the Imperial Fists effort here.'

'My most honoured lord,' the pale, half-seen phantom replied. 'I never expected that a man so great would come for us.'

'Can you, shipmistress, account for the situation as you understand it? We have precious little data. Can you give any report?'

'I have maintained my mission log since these events began,' Aquilinia replied, the edges of her words shaved off by static. 'I will link the data directly to your cogitators, so you may inload and review the information in full detail. To summarise – we were close to victory. The blisternest was under assault and due to fall. Ground forces had been despatched, and others were preparing to drop. Then the noise bursts began. You will have heard those. First the noise bursts, then the gravitational anomalies. There were not supposed to be any hazards of that sort in this system,

but they ripped through the planet's nearspace like a plague infection. One of them opened in my starboard drive and crippled us. Saved us, too.'

'Explain, please, *Amkulon*,' instructed the Lord Commander Militant.

'It nearly brought us down. We had to drop our personnel and troop strengths by boat and teleport. But I managed to arrest our descent by ejecting the damaged core, and we were able to withdraw to a safer high anchor point above the planet where we began repairs. As a result, we were the only vessel a great deal further out when the full gravitational storm erupted. It destroyed the fleet, my lord. I saw ships torn apart, and others fall on fire into the planet. I saw the *Lanxium* die.'

'Great God-Emperor!' Heth whispered.

'We were far enough out to survive the worst of it, but we were caught inside the wash of the storm, and blinded. All directional input was lost, sir. I could not move for fear of running directly into Ardamantua. I could not move until the sound of your voices showed me which direction was *out*.'

The battered *Amkulon* was still pulling clear of the worst spatial distortion. Debris trailed out behind it, whipping back into the gravity well like silver dust. Resolution on the communication image was improving, and the vox quality had got cleaner.

'The *Amkulon* was transporting Lotus Gate Company,' said Maskar to the Lord Commander.

'Shipmistress?' called Heth. 'Did Lotus Gate Company get clear, or are they still with you?'

'At my instruction,' she replied, 'they teleported to the surface. I personally gave Captain Severance the teleport locator wand so that I could recall them if the situation improved. But I lost all contact with the surface. Sir, I did not even know where the surface was. I have kept the locator's transmission signal on automatic recall, but I fear the captain and his wall are lost to us.'

They could see her on the hololith now. Her bridge was a charred ruin behind her. The image distortion had cleared somewhat, but part of what they had first taken as distortion remained. Shipmistress Aquilinia, and those members of her command crew who were in view, were all swathed head-to-foot in white cloth. It was stained in patches, as if pink fluid was gradually seeping out from within.

'Radiation burns,' muttered Kiran. 'Sweet Throne, I've never seen such extensive... They've shrouded themselves in protective veils, but they are burned, burned so badly...'

'Shipmistress,' Heth announced. 'We are sending rescue boats to you. Medicae teams will–'

'Negative,' she said. Her voice was quiet but firm. 'We are thoroughly and lethally irradiated, my lord. All of us, poisoned and scorched. We will not survive long. My entire ship is contaminated by the drive damage and utterly deadly. No one must come aboard. To board us is a death sentence.'

'But–' Heth protested.

'You have dragged us from the flames, sir, but we do not have long to live. Stay away. All I can do for you now is present my testament of events and convey all the information I have.'

'I won't accept that, shipmistress!' cried Heth.

'You must, my lord. A great disaster has overtaken the Imperial Fists here at Ardamantua.'

'We can plainly see,' said Kiran, 'a cosmic event, a gravitational hazard that–'

'It is not natural, admiral,' said the shipmistress through the vox-link.

'Say again?'

'It is not a natural phenomenon. Ardamantua has not killed us all because of some whim of the universe. This effect is artificial. This location is under direct attack.'

'Attack?' echoed Maskar.

'By what? By the Chromes? The xenoforms?' asked Heth.

'I do not believe so, sir,' answered Aquilinia. 'There are alien voices in the noise bursts. Listen to them. And watch the rising moon.'

'Ardamantua has no moon,' said Kiran.

'It does now,' said the shipmistress.

# TWENTY-ONE

## Ardamantua – orbital

'That simply cannot be a moon,' said the *Azimuth*'s First Navigator, studying the large printout that had been unfolded on the silver display tables of the charting room. 'It is far, far too close to the planet itself. Look, it is within the very aura of the nearspace disruption. That close, its gravitational effects would split Ardamantua in two.'

'Am I honestly hearing this?' asked Heth. 'We have what appears to be best described as a full-blown gravity storm besetting this planet and coring out the heart of the system, gravitational anomalies all around the nearspace region, and you say–'

'My lord,' said the First Navigator. 'I am quite precise. The gravitational incidents, the disruptions that we are seeing, are considerable. But it is random and it seems to be manufactured by distortions in space. If a planetoid appeared in such close proximity to the world, it would be a much more focused and significant effect. Ardamantua would have shifted in its orbit, perhaps even been knocked headlong.

The hazard we are encountering is like sustained damage from a shotgun. A moon... that would be a blow from a power hammer.'

'But still,' said Maskar, tapping his finger on the oddly shaded part of the printout. 'This... What is this?'

'An imaging artifact,' said the First Navigator.

'It's of considerable size,' said Maskar.

'It's a considerably sized imaging artifact, then, sir.'

'The *Amkulon* was an imaging artifact too,' Heth reminded them quietly. 'Then it turned out to be a ship.'

'The physical laws of the universe would simply not permit a moon or other satellite body to move so close to a planet, nor could such a body appear–'

'I've seen daemons,' Heth growled. 'Up close. Don't talk to me about the physical laws of the universe.'

They stood in silence and stared down at the huge printout. The chart room was cool and well-lit, arranged for the study of cosmological documents. The air circulator stirred the edges of the vast vellum sheet that hung over the edges of the silver table.

None of the ships in Kiran's fleet had been able to detect or resolve anything resembling a moon in the gravitational and radioactive maelstrom surrounding Ardamantua. The printout image had come from the mission log data transmitted to them from the *Amkulon*. Aquilinia had recorded and stored the auspex scan as she dragged her ship out of its death-dive. This had been shortly before the tumult increased, swallowed her up, and blinded her.

'We have examined the resolution,' said one of the several tech-adepts assembled in the chamber. 'The so-called "moon image" is indeed a ghost. Verifiable data is hard to find, of course, but that object seems to be only partly material, as if it is an echo of something not quite there.'

'An imaging artifact!' the First Navigator declared.

'No, sir,' said the tech-adept. 'It is like something trying to emerge. To pass through. To translate. As if through a warp gate.'

'Hellsteeth!' cried Heth. 'Then who or what are we dealing with?'

'I don't know,' said Admiral Kiran, 'but I place my full-throated support behind your efforts to pursue this, sir, rather than giving it up as a dismal and lost cause. We must find out what is happening here, and who has wrought it. Because if they can move a planetary body here, then they can pretty much move one anywhere, and do *anything*.'

# TWENTY-TWO

## Terra – the Imperial Palace

The meeting done, Wienand dismissed the four interrogators. They rose from their seats, bowed to her, raised their hoods, and left the tower-top chamber.

The Inquisitorial Representative sat alone with her thoughts for a while. There were documents and advisories to review, and her rubricator had been urging her to annotate the latest watch list.

Time enough for all of that later. The morning's news had been grim – pretty much exactly what she had been anticipating, but grim. Her masters in the three sub-divisions of the Inquisition expected much of her, and they had set her in place among the Twelve to accomplish a great deal, but it was a complicated dance, a matter of balance and timing. The Inquisition was an instrument of the Imperium. It did not set Imperial policy.

Unless it knew best, in which case it could not be *seen* to set Imperial policy.

Wienand's quarters were an eight-level suite in the

armoured crown of a tower overlooking Bastion Ledge and the Water Gardens. There was not much of a view because of the tower's ample fortification. Agents of the Inquisition had added defences of a more specialised nature when the tower was acquired for the Representative's use. The very walls and the armourglass of the windows were threaded with protective wards woven from molecular silver fibres, and potent runes had been discreetly worked into the patterns of decorative ornamentation on the carpets and ceilings. Automatic weapon arrays and intruder denial systems had been retrofitted into every staircase, doorway and floorspace, and most of the servitors were wired for weapon activation at a moment's notice. The suite was cloaked, in addition, by multiple counter-surveillance fields, and several more exotic effects derived from the esoteric arts that the Inquisition both practised and guarded against. A cone of silence, psychically generated yet psychically opaque, covered the uppermost storeys, and there was even a Mars-built, engine-rated void shield in the tower core that could be activated by voice command.

Wienand rose to her feet. She was dressed in a simple, full-length gown of pale grey wool. Her rosette adorned her wrist, as a bracelet. She felt she should summon her rubricator and begin the day's correspondence, but she was enjoying the solitude, the calm emptiness of the room.

She walked to the side table beside her desk and poured herself a glass of water from the fluted crystal jug, wishing her mind were as clear as the cool water. She raised the glass to her lips.

'There really could be anything in that, you know.'

Wienand tried not to react. She maintained her composure with an extraordinary, invisible effort. Without sipping, she set the glass down again and returned to her seat at the desk without making any eye contact, or any outward show that there should be anything troubling in the fact that Drakan Vangorich was suddenly sitting in one of the seats vacated by the interrogators.

'Such as?' she asked, moving some papers.

'Oh, toxins,' said Vangorich. 'I hear toxins are very popular. Untraceable, of course. Not necessarily lethal, but certainly mood-altering, or behaviour-modifying. Toxins that make you compliant and suggestible. Toxins that render you open to autohypnotic implanting. All sorts of things.'

'I see.'

'Don't you have a taster? An official taster? I thought you would have. A person like you.'

'I'll recruit one if it makes you happy,' she said.

'I'm only concerned for you. For a friend.'

She looked at him, directly. He was smiling, and the smile did not sit well with his scar.

'Why? Did you place a toxin in my water, Drakan?'

He shook his head.

'Throne, no. No, no. Why would I? What an awful thought.'

He paused, and looked her in the eyes.

'But I could have done. Anyone could have done, that's my point.'

'No one could have, Drakan.'

'Why is that?' he asked sweetly.

'Because no one–'

She broke off.

'Because no one can get in here?' he asked. 'Well, I seem to put the lie to that.'

He rose to his feet.

'You really are the most composed person, Wienand. Applause for that. Not even the courtesy of mild surprise at finding me here.'

'I should not be surprised,' she said.

'Even though your security advisor told you that this suite had a triple-aquila secure rating that nothing short of a primarch could get past?'

She didn't blink.

'I was quoting directly from his written report submitted for your approval nine months ago.'

'I know.'

'Page eighteen, line twenty-four.'

'If you say so.'

'Quite a colourful turn of phrase... "Nothing short of a primarch..." though not terribly technical.'

'I agree.'

'And not terribly accurate,' he said.

'I noticed.'

'I'd sack him, if I were you.'

'Drakan,' she said, done with his games, 'I'm impressed. All right? Does that satisfy you? I'm impressed that you got in here without setting off any alarm or countermeasure. It is almost inhumanly chilling that you were able to do so.'

'Thank you,' he replied. 'For what it's worth, when it comes to the private Palace apartments of the High Twelve, this is by far the hardest to get into.'

He looked at her and affected an expression of innocence.

'So I'm told,' he said.

'I presume you came here for a purpose,' she said.

He sat down again, leaned back and crossed his legs.

'I *presume*,' he echoed, 'that you read the transcripts this morning?'

'In particular?' she asked.

He sighed.

'You're really going to make me work for it, aren't you?' he asked. 'The first intercepts are back from Heth's valiant rescue mission. Ardamantua is a mess. Worse than could be imagined. The sheer scale of the loss isn't yet reckoned, nor is the true nature of the threat. But... it's bad news.'

'Yes, I saw that,' Wienand replied.

'You're very calm about it,' he observed.

'There's no point panicking,' she answered. 'There's every point making a considered and rational response. It is a threat. A severe threat.'

'Just as you originally suggested,' he said. 'That's why I thought I'd come and have a little word with you. You used me slightly, Wienand. You used me to move against Lansung in the Senatorum. That's fine. I quite enjoyed it. It's nice to feel wanted. You were concerned about the threat, because no one seemed to be taking it particularly seriously, but you were far more concerned with Lansung and his power bloc of allies, and the way the threat – and others like it – might be mishandled by them. It was a political manoeuvre to realign the High Lords. That's how you sold it to me.'

'Agreed. So?'

'The threat's very, very real, Wienand. It's not a valid excuse for brokering, it's a palpable problem. And I think you knew it was when you co-opted me. What does the Inquisition know that the rest of us don't?'

'I was concerned with Lansung's high-handed attitude towards–'

Vangorich raised a hand.

'There is a threat to the Imperium that is of far greater magnitude than anyone imagines, but the Inquisition is reluctant to disclose it. Instead, the Inquisition attempts to use political subterfuge to alter Imperial doctrine and policy.'

'Not so,' she said.

'One would hope not, or that might be regarded very badly. The Inquisition taking over effective control of Imperial policy? There's a word for that.'

'A word?'

'The word is "coup".'

'Drakan,' she said, 'you're beginning to frustrate me with your paranoia. The Inquisition is not attempting to mount a political coup from within the Senatorum.'

'Well,' he replied, 'it would seem to be one thing or the other. Either the Inquisition is trying to take control because it knows something the rest of us don't, or you really are very concerned at the fitness of Lansung and his kind to sit at the high table.'

She said nothing.

'What is the threat, Wienand?'

'It is what it is.'

'What is the nature of the threat?'

'You know as much as I do, Grand Master. It is a xenos threat that requires attention.'

He rose again.

'So you're sticking to your story. This is all about your concern about power balance and the fitness of Lansung, Udo and the others to rule?'

She nodded.

'Well, that rather makes it my problem, then, doesn't it? An issue for my Officio?'

'What do you mean?' she asked, with a slight note of anxiety.

'Well, if any High Lord is deemed by his peers to be unfit or unworthy, the ultimate sanction has always been the Officio Assassinorum. It's why we exist. It is our purview. Political subterfuge is entirely a waste of time when you have the Officio to clean house.'

'Vangorich, don't be medieval.'

He leaned on her desk and stared into her face.

'Then I suggest you start trusting me,' he said. 'Tell me the nature of this threat. Share it with all of us. Tell me what is so terrible. What scares the Inquisition so much it needs to take control of Imperial policy? What do you know?'

She stared back at him, and hesitated.

Then she said, 'There's nothing. Nothing to tell.'

He stood up straight.

'I see,' he said. 'I see. If that's all you'll say, I see I must take you at your word. I suppose I had better get about my business.'

'What does that mean?' she asked. 'Drakan, what are you suggesting?'

He walked to her side table, picked up the glass of water she had poured, and drank it down.

'I'm not suggesting anything,' he said. 'I am going about my business and performing the duties entrusted to me.'

He walked towards the door.

'Drakan,' she called after him. 'Don't do anything. Don't do anything foolish. Please. This situation is very sensitive. This moment... You mustn't act rashly.'

'I'll try not to,' he replied. 'But if no one tells me where the sensitivities lie, I cannot help but step on them, can I?'

The door opened, and Wienand's bodyguard Kalthro strode in, a pistol raised. He halted when he saw Vangorich.

'Far too little,' Vangorich told him as he strode past, 'far too late.'

# TWENTY-THREE

### Ardamantua

Daylight led the way over the broken ridge and down into the rubble-strewn valley where the lake spread out under a black sky. His armour, and the plate armour of the other three Imperial Fists, was spattered with ichor. No one had made any attempt to clean it off. They had left the field on the other side of the ridge strewn with dead xenos, piled high. It had plainly astonished Major Nyman and the Asmodai troopers, who had moved in towards the end and helped to slay the last few dozen with targeted fire.

Gravity, shifting and flexing like an invisible serpent through earth and air, shattered a distant row of hills with a noise like thunder. The clouds boiled past overhead, on fast-play. Flames of red, green and yellow danced around the ridges of broken rock and upturned, split earth.

'Once we reach the lake, then what?' asked Bastion Ledge.

'From the lake, the nest,' replied Daylight.

'Then?' Bastion Ledge asked.

'Then we look for survivors,' replied Daylight. 'For signs.'

'And if we find none?'

'We look elsewhere.'

'And if more of those things appear?' Bastion Ledge asked.

'Then we kill more of those things,' said Daylight.

They skirted a series of murky pools and crooked ponds that were offshoots of the lake, their trudging figures reflected in the water, the running sky behind them. The wind blew. The noise bursts continued to break the air, howling barks that came from everywhere and nowhere.

The gravity blister popped without any warning except a slight shrug of physical matter. A random anomaly, it opened on the edge of one of the pools about fifty metres from their procession. The physicality of the world, the rocks, the air and the pool altered instantaneously. It went off like a bomb, hurling tonnes of stone and soil into the air sideways, like a blizzard. The ground broke open and water turned to steam. The main volume of the pool surged in the opposite direction in a spontaneous tidal wave three metres tall, and broke across the next ridge with enough force to shatter rock.

Flying rocks and debris, along with mud and water, ripped along the line of Daylight's party. The Guardsmen were knocked off their feet. One died, his head crushed by a boulder. Only the frail, mind-addled tech-adept, bewildered and confused, remained upright.

Rocks and stones rained off the Imperial Fists, pelting their armour. In that instant, Daylight once again felt the uneasy fear. The Imperial Fists excelled at holding ground, but how did a warrior do that when the ground itself couldn't be trusted?

The thought barely had time to form before another blister

ripped the world open. It was smaller than the first, a gravitic aftershock, but it was right under them. Two of the
Asmodai simply atomised, turning into clouds of blood and
whizzing armour shreds, their forms lost in the explosive
upchuck of rock and bludgeoning concussion.

Bastion Ledge died too.

As the smoke and steam cleared, and the last of the rock
debris rained down and skittered around them, as the ground
stopped shaking, Daylight saw his wall-brother. Half of Bastion Ledge, most of the left-hand side of his body, was missing.
It was folded and compressed in on itself, flesh, bone and
armour alike. He looked as though he had been snatched up
by a giant and squeezed until he was crushed like a tin cup.
Black blood drenched his buckled, ruined wargear.

Zarathustra knelt beside him to check for vitals, but they
all knew it was in vain. Bastion was gone, killed by the
world, killed by the ground, killed by the forces of nature
they ought to have been able to trust.

For a second, Daylight felt hopelessness, but there was
no time to consider such luxuries as emotions.

A third gravity blister blew out on the far side of the valley,
and the *boom* rolled around the outcrops. It hardly mat-
tered. There was a more immediate threat.

Major Nyman was shouting. He'd ripped his helmet off so
he could be heard and he was yelling, gasping in the thin air.

Daylight turned.

Chromes were coming out of the stretch of lake behind
them, scrambling towards the shore. They were all large,
dark, mature and powerful. Flying rocks hurled by the
third gravity detonation hammered across the lake, killing

several of them and sending up spouts of water, as though heavy-calibre gunfire were peppering the surface. The Chromes churned on regardless, bounding up the stony shore to attack the Imperial party.

Nyman and his men began to fire, though some of the Asmodai were still dazed from the triple hammerblow of the gravity blisters. Zarathustra sprang up and charged down the slope into the water, impaling first one and then a second dark Chrome with his war-spear. He felled a third with a savage back-thrust of the spear's haft, and then threw himself full-length to tackle a Chrome in the shallows that was bearing down on Major Nyman. Nyman's repeated shots were not slowing it down. Zarathustra knocked the creature sideways, and then tangled into a wrestling brawl with it, kicking up sprays of froth and water.

Tranquility used his boltgun as he moved down the shore, picking off two more of the Chromes that had come too close to the Asmodai line. His mass-reactive shells stopped them dead in a way that the poor Guardsmen's las-rounds could not. It took sustained, saturating fire to stop a warrior-form with a lasrifle. Having bought enough time with his shots to get at the Chromes close-quarters, Tranquility holstered his bolter and unslung the power hammer from his backplate. He crushed one Chrome's skull down into its shoulders and then struck another sideways, into the shallows. Its cranium split and ichor sprayed out. A third, attacking the Imperial Fist furiously, was knocked back with the butt of the haft, leaving it open for a downward smash of the head that ruptured it like a well-cooked piece of shellfish.

Ichor stained the frothing surface of the lake at the shallows.

Daylight met the attack with his gladius in his right hand and his combat knife in his left. He stabbed his sword through a sternum plate, and then slashed a mouth and throat open with his knife. As his second kill fell back, Daylight used the combat knife to block the striking claws of a third Chrome warrior-form, shoved the creature's limbs up and aside, and ripped his sword through its exposed midriff with a sideways slash.

A fourth Chrome closed. Daylight outstepped its charge and hacked his sword edge into its spine as it passed him, dropping it on its face into the pool. A fifth beast ran onto his extended knife. A sixth died from a cross cut, a double slash of both weapons that ran from shoulders to hips.

A particularly large Chrome seized Daylight from behind, sawing into his armour with its claws, gnawing into his backplate with its mouthparts. It hoisted him off his feet, backwards, tilting.

Daylight inverted his grip on both blades, letting them fall out of his hands so he could catch them again reversed, and then stabbed past either side of his hips with the sword and the knife, impaling the torso that was braced against his. The Chrome burst at the wound points and sprayed ichor. It collapsed, pulling Daylight down with it into the water in a thrashing commotion.

Others rushed at him, trying to rip into the Imperial Fists wall-brother before he could regain his footing. Zarathustra and some of the Asmodai saw this and moved to support. The Guardsmen fired at the thrashing Chromes, and Zarathustra charged them, spear raised.

Gunfire raked the surface of the pool, cutting down

dozens of the Chromes. It resembled the fury of spume and spouts that had been kicked up by the rock debris, but it was real gunfire.

Rotor cannons.

Tranquility turned.

Zarathustra reached Daylight and hauled him upright, stabbing at the Chromes that tried to mob and menace them.

Figures moved down the stony shore towards them, a squad of men. Two in the lead carried rotor cannons, firing bursts into the pool as they approached to drive back the xenoforms.

They were Imperial Fists.

Daylight crunched up the shoreline out of the water to meet them, Zarathustra at his heels.

The squad commander faced them, and removed his helm.

'Severance, captain, Lotus Gate Wall,' he said. 'Where did you come from?'

# TWENTY-FOUR

## Ardamantua

'We've been on the surface six weeks,' said Severance. 'At least, I presume it's about that long. Gravity distortion is so prolific planetside, I feel we can't trust any other laws. Several suit chronometers are showing significant time variances. This world is not aligned with the natural flow of the cosmos.'

'Increasingly so,' Daylight agreed. 'Six weeks is a reasonable estimate. We've been in transit roughly that long, from Terra.'

'Who's with you?' asked Severance.

'Everything that was left. The *Phalanx* is emptied and the walls of the Palace are bare. We've got a decent fleet support, and a substantial Guard cohort.'

Severance shook his head.

'I can't believe we've left the walls bare. I can't. If Mirhen...'

'Does the beloved Chapter Master still live?' asked Daylight.

Severance shrugged.

'My wall made an emergency drop to the surface via teleport when the *Amkulon* was holed. It was an extreme measure, and I would rather not have abandoned the vessel.'

Daylight saw that Captain Severance carried a battered teleport locator on his harness. A power light showed that it was still, futilely, activated.

'By the time we were down, we were blind,' Severance continued. 'The gravity storm had closed in. We've been scouring the surface for survivors or contacts ever since. We saw drop-ships. Stormbirds? That's what brought us this way.'

'You must have been in the vicinity already,' said Zarathustra.

'Yes,' said Severance. 'We managed to identify this zone, despite the geological upheavals, as the site of the original blisternest, so my wall has been section-searching the area to look for survivors.'

'And ammunition,' remarked Severance's second-in-command, Merciful. His tone was mordant.

Daylight smiled. He was amused that both he and Severance had independently lighted on the same strategy. It reassured him that the core training of the Chapter was both profound and reliable.

'Have you found anything?' asked Zarathustra.

'A few pitiful dead,' replied Merciful. 'Crushed by the tormented planet or overthrown by the Chromes.'

'They're not the real enemy,' said Severance.

'What do you mean?' asked Tranquility.

'The Chromes are just a hazard, and the cause of our undertaking here,' Severance replied. 'But there's something else. Something that wasn't here before. You can feel it. You can hear its voice on the wind.'

As if to underscore his remark, noise bursts echoed across the valley.

'Substantiate that,' said Daylight very directly.

'I cannot,' Severance replied. 'It's a gut feeling.'

'The walls do not deal in gut feelings,' said Daylight. 'The shield-corps relies on what is verifiable.'

He looked at Severance uneasily. Perhaps the brother had been here too long, subjected to the extremities of the environment. Perhaps gravity, or one of the other natural or even unnatural forces being twisted and convoluted on Ardamantua, had affected his personality or his brain chemistry. Where Daylight had felt reassured by the overlap of their tactical decisions, he now felt a distance, as if the bond of the shield and wall did not connect them at all.

'Have you seen the shape in the sky?' Severance asked.

'What? No,' said Daylight.

'Some things cannot be substantiated,' said Severance. He rose from where he had been sitting on the boulders scattered at the shore and gestured Daylight to follow him. Daylight did so reluctantly. The pair clambered up an outcrop overlooking the dark mirror of the lake.'

'Wait,' said Severance. 'Look.'

'At what? What am I looking at? The sky?'

'No, look at the lake.'

'You asked if I had seen the thing in the sky–'

'Be patient, Daylight. It comes and goes.'

They waited. Daylight felt he was wasting valuable time.

'Look,' said Severance.

The scudding, racing cloud-cover, moving across the heavens like a black lava flow, parted briefly, riven by the wind and orbital disruption. Sunlight speared through in a pale beam. The sky beyond the cloud was white and blank, like static. There was nothing to be seen.

But in the lake...

Daylight started. It was there and gone in an instant, but he had seen it. He reset his visor recorder for immediate playback, and then froze the image.

Therein, the clouds were parted, drawn like drapes to show a colourless sky where nothing resided. In the reflection below, however, trapped in the surface of the lake, the patch of bright sky did contain something.

Something large and ominous, an orb that seemed to press down on the wounded planet.

It was a moon. A black, ungodly, hideous moon.

# TWENTY-FIVE

## Ardamantua

They had been walking around the lake edge in the company of Severance's squad for several hours when they spotted the flare.

It lofted up in the distance, an incandescently bright pin-prick, then shivered as it hung in place, before fading and falling away, all effort spent.

'One of mine!' Severance cried. 'Move!'

They began to make the best pace possible. As the leaders ran ahead, Captain Severance told Daylight that his subdivided wall had agreed to use basic flares and visual signals to stay in contact, given that everything up to and including short-range helm-to-helm vox was useless.

The ragged Asmodai troopers couldn't keep up. Major Nyman had put his helmet back on, exhausted by the impure air, but rather more troubled by the constant noise bursts. Even those Asmodai who had kept the visors of their orbital drop-suits firmly sealed since planetfall were feeling the effects. The noise bursts echoed into the cavities of

their helmets and armour, unsettling them. It was psycho-
logically hammering them.

Severance pointed to four of his men and told them to
stay with the Guardsmen and bring them along behind.
Then he set out at full pace.

It took them half an hour to reach the origin of the signal flare. Daylight was beside Severance as they slowed to
approach.

It was a second search party from Lotus Gate Wall, com-
manded by a sergeant called Diligent.

'Good to see you, sir,' the sergeant called out. He hesitated
as he saw Daylight and the other Space Marines new to him.

'I see you've made discoveries of your own,' he remarked.

'What did you find?' asked Severance.

'The blisternest, or what's left of it,' said Diligent. 'And
survivors.'

The survivors of the original undertaking assault had taken
shelter in the ruins of the blisternest, using its structure
to weather out the worst the gravity storms threw at them.
They had, in the weeks since, constructed a makeshift stockade from boulders, wreckage and parts of the nest structure.

Inside the jagged walls, there were men from Ballad Gateway, Hemispheric, Anterior Six Gate and Daylight walls,
about one hundred and thirty of them all told, together with
a few, fragile servitors. There was no substantial equipment,
no heavy weapons or vehicles with them, and precious little munitions supply.

First Captain Algerin of Hemispheric had command.

'Well met in bad days,' he said to Severance and Daylight.

He looked at Daylight, and at Tranquility and Zarathustra nearby.

'You left the walls unguarded to come for us? I'm not sure I approve.'

'You're not the first person to express that thought, captain,' said Daylight. 'We made our choice. The Chapter was beset.'

'Worse than beset,' said Algerin. His voice dropped. 'Worse than beset.'

He looked at the ground. His armour was almost black with filth, and it showed hundreds of nicks and gouges from Chrome claws.

'The Chapter Master is dead,' he said, aiming each word like a las-bolt at the ground. 'He reached the surface by teleport before the flagship was lost. He came to us. He was with us for three weeks. Chromes took him. Rent him. There were three hundred of us then. They wear us down. There are so many of them. Attrition, the coward's tactic.'

Algerin looked at them.

'He was so angry,' he said. 'Mirhen, such a great man, but so *angry*. He railed at the gods, at the stars, to see his fleet wrecked and his Chapter shredded, and the honour that has carried us through at the forefront of all Chapters, since the very start, shredded away... by animals. By vermin and a crooked planet.'

He took a breath.

'They killed him because of his anger, you know,' he said. 'He wanted to kill them. He wanted to kill them all, but there were too many. I tried to pull him back. He–'

Algerin stopped. He looked at Daylight.

'You have brought ships to take us off here, wall-brother?' he asked.

'I have,' replied Daylight. 'But conditions are still bad. We have to devise a way for them to get close enough to effect evac.'

'I don't think conditions will improve,' said Algerin. 'Not any time soon.'

He looked up as Severance's men brought the Asmodai stragglers into the makeshift fortification.

'Men,' he said, unimpressed. 'They will not last long. We had about fifty auxiliaries with us at the start. The noises drove them mad in the first week. We had to... It wasn't a good situation. Only one of them survived. I suspect it's because he was scatter-brained to begin with. He's determined though, I'll give him that. Determined to puzzle it out.'

'What do you mean?' asked Daylight.

'See for yourself,' Algerin invited. 'He's with one of yours.'


'I am Slaughter,' said the second captain of Daylight Wall Company.

'I am... Daylight,' said Daylight.

'I'm glad of the sight of you,' said Slaughter. 'You came for us. That won't be forgotten.'

Daylight nodded. 'I am heartened to hear that sentiment from one mouth at least. Who is your charge here?' he asked. A bedraggled and filthy human in ragged robes was hunkered in the corner of the nest chamber, working at various pieces of Imperial apparatus. The devices, stacked and piled against the chamber wall, many of them damaged, were running off battery power. Several of them had clearly been customised, refitted, or repurposed.

'He is the magos biologis sent to accompany our mission,' Slaughter explained. The chamber was gloomy and dank, part of the surviving underground burrows of the blister-nest. Water dripped from the organic arch of the roof.

'He was supposed to study the xenoforms while we killed them. I was set to guard him when our fortunes changed. I've been doing that ever since, pretty much.'

They approached the scientist. He was intent on his work, muttering to himself. He was in need of a decent shave. His hair, dirty and unruly, had been clipped back in a bunch using the bent clasp of an ammunition pack.

'His name is Laurentis,' said Slaughter.

'Magos,' said Daylight, crouching beside the magos biologis. 'Magos? I am Daylight.'

Laurentis looked at him for a moment.

'Oh, a new one,' he said. 'You're new. He's new, Slaughter. See? See, there? I'm beginning to tell you apart.'

He smiled.

Noise bursts echoed outside the chamber, and Laurentis winced and rubbed his ears roughly with begrimed knuckles.

'The wavelength is changing. It's changing. Today, and these last few days. Greater intensity. Yes, greater intensity.'

The magos biologis looked at them as if they might understand.

'I had specialist equipment,' he said. 'I was sent it by the Chapter Master himself...'

He paused, and thought, his eyes darkening.

'He's dead now, isn't he?'

'Yes,' said Slaughter.

'Well, yes. Sad. Anyway, before that happened, him, dying, he sent me equipment. I asked him for it. Specialist equipment. I asked for it, you see? But so much of it was damaged before I could use it. Everything went a bit crazy. Yes, a bit crazy.'

'The magos believed from the very outset,' Slaughter said to Daylight, 'that the noise bursts were a form of communication. He wanted to decipher them. A drop of specialist equipment to allow him to do that was arranged, but it had been overrun by Chromes and half-scrapped by the time we got to it.'

'Communication,' said Daylight. 'From the Chromes?'

'I thought so at first,' said Laurentis, jumping up suddenly to stretch his cramping legs. 'Yes, yes, I did. At first. I thought we had underestimated the technical abilities of the Chromes. I thought we had underestimated their sapience. They migrate from world to world. That suggested a great capacity for... for, uhm...'

Another noise burst, a longer one, had just echoed though the darkness of the stockade and the ruined nest, and it had rather distracted him.

'What was I saying?' he asked them, digging his knuckles into his ears again and jiggling his head.

'Communication?' prompted Daylight. He remembered very clearly what had been spoken of on the bridge of the *Azimuth*. The noises coming from Ardamantua read as organic – boosted and amplified for broadcast, but organic. Like a voice. 'You believe it's communication?' he pressed.

'Yes! Yes! That's what I thought! That was my theory, and it seemed a valid one. I thought the Chromes were trying to surrender, or negotiate peace, that's what I thought at first. Do you remember me saying that, Slaughter?'

'I do, magos,' said Slaughter.

'Then I thought they might be trying to compose a challenge. Then I thought they might be warning us, you know, *warning* us not to mess with them. Then, then I thought they might be trying to warn us about something else.'

'Like what?' asked Daylight.

'Well,' said Laurentis, 'it doesn't much matter, because I don't believe it is them at all any more. Do I, Slaughter?'

'You don't,' said Slaughter.

'I think it's someone else. Yes, that's what I think. Someone *else*.'

The magos biologis looked at them both.

'What do you think?' he asked.

'I think I'd like you to explain more,' said Daylight. 'Who do you think this someone else is?'

Laurentis shrugged.

'Someone very advanced,' he said. 'Very advanced. Take gravity, for example. They are very, very advanced in that field. Gravitic engineering! Imagine! They're shifting something. And this world, it's just the delivery point.'

'What are they shifting?'

'Something very big,' said Laurentis.

'A moon?' asked Daylight. Slaughter looked at him sharply.

'It could be a moon. Yes, it could be,' said Laurentis. 'You've seen the reflection in the lake, have you?'

'I have,' said Daylight.

'Whatever it is, it's still in transition. If it's a moon or a planetoid... well, Throne save us all. That's a different class of everything. I mean, we can terraform, we can even realign small planetoids in-system. But shifting planetary bodies on an interstellar range? That's... *god-like*. There are rumours, of course. Stories. Myths. They say that the ancients, the precursor races, they say they had power of that magnitude. Even the eldar once, at the very peak of their culture. But not any more. No one can do that any more. Not on that scale.'

'Except... whoever the voice belongs to?' asked Daylight.

'Yes, well, perhaps,' said Laurentis.

'And who does the voice belong to?' asked Daylight.

Noises boomed and howled. Laurentis scrabbled at his ears again like a man with headlice, and pulled a pained face.

'That's the real trick, isn't it?' he agreed. 'Knowing that. Knowing that thing. We'd have to translate the words first, and find out what they were saying. Maybe... maybe they're introducing themselves to us? Maybe this is a contact message. A hello. I've spent six weeks trying to figure that out...'

He made a sweeping gesture that encompassed his make-shift pile of devices and equipment.

'...six weeks, working with these items, which are hardly ideal. It's so hard to jury-rig what I'm missing. The parsing cogitators are a particular loss. And the vocalisation monitors. I've made do with quite a lot, actually, quite a lot, but Throne alive! What I wouldn't give for a decent grade tech-servitor, or a vox-servitor... or... or an augmetic receiver. Cranial! Cranial implants! I never took them myself, you see?'

'If this is contact,' asked Daylight, 'it's surely hostile?'

Laurentis nodded, blinking away another noise burst with a shake of his head. 'I mean, definitely. Definitely. But it would still be worth hearing what it had to say for itself.'

'You would confirm a hostile intent, then?'

'I don't have to!' Laurentis exclaimed. 'Look at the rats!'

'The rats?' asked Daylight.

'No, not rats. The Chromes. That's what I mean. The Chromes. *Like* rats. You can gather so much data by observing the behaviour patterns and habits of animals. Rats. Remember when I first called them rats, Slaughter? Remember that?'

'I do, magos,' said Slaughter.

'I said it as a joke, at first,' said Laurentis. 'I said it because their behaviour reminded me of rat behaviour. Rats suddenly turning hostile and flooding into a new area with great and uncharacteristic aggression. It can be very scary. Very dangerous. They're not a threat. They live under the floorboards and in the walls for years, never harming anyone, and then they are turned into a threat. *Turned into* one!'

'How?' asked Daylight.

'Because *they* are threatened, by a greater natural predator. Something they fear. Yes, fear enough to make them attack things they would not normally attack. In this case, the Imperium. And Space Marines! Goodness me, the Chromes are just animals. They are just vermin! They're rats, rats, you see? We're fighting them because they've been driven into our zones of space by something they do not want to be around. They are fleeing, fleeing for their lives, and it's made them desperate enough to battle us.'

He looked at them both.

'It makes sense, doesn't it?' he asked, pleased with himself. He grinned. Daylight noticed that, at some point, several of the magos biologis' teeth had been knocked out. The gappy smile made him look more like an eager child than a credible expert.

'If they're animals, how are they travelling between worlds?' asked Daylight. 'How are they effecting interstellar and void transport?'

Laurentis clapped his hands and did a little jig.

'That's another thing, you see? You see? That's sort of what clinches it because it neatly answers the other mystery! How do the Chromes get from world to world? How do they migrate? What explains their diaspora? Nothing! They can't do it! They're animals! QED something is bringing them here! They're moving through the tunnels!'

'The... tunnels?' asked Daylight.

'Yes. Tunnels. There's probably a better word for it. I haven't really worked this material up into a presentation form yet. Tunnels will have to do. The tunnels built by whoever the voice belongs to.'

He looked at Slaughter, and then Daylight, then back to Slaughter.

'Whoever owns the voice,' he said quietly, as though someone might overhear, 'is equipped with a highly superior tech level. They can manipulate, at a fundamental level, gravity and other primary forces of the universe. They can, so it would appear, reposition planetary bodies over interstellar distances. They do this by constructing tunnels – let's use that word – tunnels through space. Perhaps through the warp itself, as we understand it – not that we *really* understand it, mind – or through some closely associated stratum of subspace. Perhaps a gravitational sublayer, or even a teleportational vector. I can't really be sure yet, so let's simply settle on the term "subspace tunnel", shall we? Now the Chromes, they're vermin, you see? Pests? They live in that subspace realm we're talking about. Like rats live in an attic or a sewer. The subspace realm is an attic of the universe we don't ever see. A cosmic sewer. And as the owner of the voice moves through that attic... subspace realm... you still with me? As the owner of the voice does that, it drives them ahead of it.'

'The Chromes are spread indirectly,' said Daylight, 'via the transportational rifts constructed by this... unknown xenoform.'

'Very well put!' Laurentis exclaimed. 'Can I write that down? Like rats in an attic that's on fire, the Chromes are being driven out ahead of the flames, fighting anything that gets in their way. Or like rats in a sewer, where there are big lizards of some sort, and the big lizards are trying to eat them, so they're afraid and they're running away from the big lizards and–'

'I get it,' said Daylight. 'Calm yourself, magos.'

He looked over at Slaughter.

'We very much need to find out what's coming, captain,' he said.

Slaughter nodded.

'It's not going to be pretty when it arrives,' said Laurentis, quieter now. 'It's an immense threat. The Chromes may be pests, and essentially non-sentient, but they are durable,

and resilient and highly numerous, and their entire population – whole nests, whole family communities, millions
strong – is being forced to flee for parsecs across the galaxy,
through the cellars and chimneys of space.'

He paused.

'Just like rats.'

Daylight was thinking.

'Did you say,' he asked the magos biologis suddenly, 'that
you needed a servitor? What about a tech-adept? Would a
tech-adept do?'

# TWENTY-SIX

## Ardamantua

'But his primary socket's ripped out!' Laurentis complained.

'He was hurt during the crash,' Major Nyman explained patiently. He had opened the faceplate of his atmospheric suit so he could be heard. The major clearly didn't trust the filthy, matted magos biologis at all. He was wary of his manic, agitated behaviour. 'He's been hurt. Stop manhandling him.'

'Please be calm, major,' said Daylight. 'Magos, perhaps you could be a little more gentle with the adept? He is injured and hardly in the best shape.'

'Yes, yes, of course,' Laurentis said.

Nyman and two of his Asmodai had brought the tech-adept into the magos biologis's chamber, and were helping him settle on a seat made of a munition crate beside Laurentis's repurposed workstation.

The humans had all been fed from some of the rations in the stockade's supplies. They'd been given purified water too. First Captain Algerin didn't think much of their survival odds. Humans, in his experience, had about four or five days' tolerance for the conditions of Ardamantua. Algerin also didn't seem to think much of Daylight's interest in the magos biologis' theories. To Algerin, Laurentis was an eccentric who had been driven half-mad by his prolonged exposure to the environment, and was probably fairly deranged and obsessive in the first place. 'It's a miracle he's survived this long,' Algerin had remarked, and Daylight wasn't clear if that meant Algerin was surprised that Laurentis had outlasted the other human survivors, or if he thought it was a miracle he hadn't silenced the magos long since.

The tech-adept seemed a little calmer for food and water, and also to be out of the open, in a place where the noise bursts were more muffled. Nevertheless, his eyes were still dead and wandering, and his movements jerky. The sudden attention and manic eagerness of the tattered magos made him shrink back, timid and alarmed.

The magos made soothing, cooing noises, and began to examine the ruined primary plug in the back of the tech-adept's neck. The touch of his fingers on the blood-crusted injury made the adept wince. Laurentis made a tutting sound and looked elsewhere.

'Secondary plugs,' he said, with some relief. 'Here in the sternum, and under the arms. Also the spine. Not as clean and direct as a primary cortex, but it should do the trick. Yes, very good, under the circumstances.'

He looked sidelong at Daylight and whispered, 'The fellow looks a little ropey, though, sir. A little wobbly.'

'He's been injured,' said Daylight. 'In the crash. So he might be a limited resource. He's not strong or mentally robust.'

'Crash. Right. Yes, I remember you saying that,' said Laurentis. 'I'll just have to use whatever I can.'

He began fiddling with the dirty brass dials and levers of his machinery. Oscilloscopes flashed and pulsed, and small hololithic monitors lit up, displaying angry storms of ambient noise. The relayed echoes of noise bursts and other background sonics, most of them from the upper atmosphere and nearspace, fluttered out of the speakers at low volume.

The tech-adept shivered as a series of long, low, booming noise bursts filled the air outside. He shivered again as Laurentis began to connect jack leads to his implant sockets. His eyes rolled back as the last lead plugged into his spinal augmetic and linked to his damaged cortex.

'I've had the basic parsing program complete for over a week,' Laurentis explained as he worked. 'I mean, it was relatively simple. Relatively. The problem was the lack of a decent vocalisation monitor. I basically made the translation, but I couldn't read it, you see? I couldn't read it. To read or hear the translation, you need to pass the translated data-stream through the language centres of a live cortex. The language centres sort of do the work for you. They get the signal and interpret it.'

He looked at Daylight as he adjusted some settings on the devices, and then tweaked the fit of the adept's sternum plug.

'I thought of using my own language centres,' he said pleasantly. 'That would work. Except I don't have the cranial plug. No cranial plug. There are ways around that, I suppose, but I couldn't find a knife clean enough.'

The adept suddenly stiffened. His spine went rigid. His head started to twitch.

'That's good,' said Laurentis, adjusting some dials.

'Is it really?' asked Nyman doubtfully.

'Very good,' Laurentis insisted.

He turned a gain knob, and then gently dialled up a feed source.

The tech-adept began to twitch more violently. His head rocked and jiggled, and his eyes rolled back. His mouth began to move. Saliva flecked his lips as they ground and churned, as though they were trying to form words.

'Stop it,' said Nyman.

'It's all going very well,' said Laurentis.

'I said stop it,' Nyman warned.

'Back off or get out, Major Nyman,' Daylight said.

There was a sound. A soft sound. A tiny blurt of noise. They all looked. It had come from the adept. His chewing, churning mouth, with spittle roping from it, was forming words. He was speaking.

'What was that?' asked Nyman.

'Listen to him!' Laurentis insisted.

The adept began to make louder noises. He gurgled and choked on the amorphous sound-forms and half-words bubbling out of his voicebox. The sound was coming from his throat, across his palate, as if he was enunciating something primordial, something from the dark, hindbrain portions of his mind.

It grew louder still, deeper, more brutal. It was an ugly sound, an animal sound, atavistic.

Finally, there were words.

'Did you hear that?' Laurentis cried.

'What did he say?' asked Nyman.

'Did you hear that?' Laurentis repeated, excitedly.

The tech-adept, blind, rigid and drooling, was repeating one phrase, over and over, in a deep, bass voice.

'I am Slaughter,' he was saying. 'I am Slaughter.'

'Oh, that's not right,' said the magos, suddenly disappointed. 'That's you.'

He looked at Slaughter.

'That's what you say,' said Laurentis. 'That's the thing you say. He's overheard you and he's just repeating it. Poor, mindless fool. I said he was no good. Too damaged, you see? Too damaged. Just repeating what he heard. What a pity. I had such high hopes. The whole thing's a failure.'

Slaughter looked at the tech-adept, who was still in rigour, grunting out the crude phrase.

'He's never met me,' he said. 'He's never heard me say that. He's never met me.'

# TWENTY-SEVEN

## Ardamantua – orbital

Something was happening to the nearspace shadow around Ardamantua. The gravity storm was intensifying. All the sensors and auspex arrays on the bridge of the *Azimuth* went into the red scale, and then the vermillion, and then went to white-out. Glass dials cracked and blew out of their brass mounts. Sensor servitors squealed and clutched at their aug-plugged eyes and ears, or wrenched out their cortical jacks in sprays of blood and amniotic fluid. The main strategium flickered and then died in a ribboned flurry of collapsing hololithic composition streams.

Admiral Kiran, who had been closely observing the attempts to steer the wounded *Amkulon* towards the flank of a recovery tender, leapt out of his high-backed throne. The cosmological event had accelerated so suddenly, so violently. The seething, simmering storm surrounding the target planet had, in the space of twenty or thirty seconds, turned into something else entirely. The cream of his sensory and detection bridge crew were crippled and blinded, and most of his primary range-finding and scanning apparatus was annihilated. He was quite sure that the planet was about to die. From the energetic signature dynamic, as he had briefly glimpsed it before the screens went dead, the gravity anomaly was expanding, spiking. The planet would never survive a trauma like that. Tectonic rending and seismic disruption would husk the world like a ripe crop, and squirt the molten core of Ardamantua into space in a super-cooling jet of matter.

'Shields! Shields!' he yelled, though his experienced deck crew were already enabling the *Azimuth*'s potent forward shields. Kiran hoped that the commanders of his fleet components closest to the nearspace rim would have the wit to initiate emergency evasive manoeuvres and pull back from the planet zone as rapidly as their real space drives would allow.

If the planet died, his fleet would die with it.

'What's happening?' Heth yelled, running onto the bridge in his breeches and undershirt, braces around his hips, shaving cream covering half of his chin. His aides and attendants rushed after him as if they could somehow complete his ablutions while he yelled at Kiran.

Maskar also appeared, emerging from the chart room with data-slates in his hand, a bemused expression on his face.

'We have a situation,' Kiran said, trying to pull data up onto his repeater screens. 'We have a very serious situation. Something is happening to the planet.'

He turned and yelled at the strategium officers.

'Get that thing re-lit! Get a data-feed up! I don't care if you have to act as live connectors and hold the power couplers together with your bare hands!'

They rushed to obey him, though there seemed to be little hope of restoring the feed. Sparks and filaments of shredded and burned-out cable showered from the cavernous roof of the *Azimuth*'s bridge. Several of the gleaming silver consoles had burst into flames and two large monitor plates had cracked with gunshot bangs and exploded. Servitor crews rushed forwards to extinguish the conflagrations and haul the injured crewmen away, burned and peppered with glass chippings.

Kiran's bridge crew were some of the best in the Imperial Navy. Whatever could be said about Lord High Admiral Lansung, he insisted on the highest degree of schooling for the first-line and primary battlefleet candidates. Working with the tools they had to hand, the sensorium techs managed to reconnect the strategium main display and re-engage it to half-power.

An image blinked into view, fuzzy and indistinct, flaring with distortion and interference.

'What is it? What are we looking at–' Heth began.

'Shut up!' Kiran said, flapping a hand at him and peering at the display.

'How dare you speak to the Lord Commander Militant in that–' Maskar exclaimed.

'You shut up too!' Kiran bellowed, his eyes never leaving the strategium display. 'Look! Look at the damned display!'

In the hololith, the orb of Ardamantua was buckling and shuddering, surrounded by a vast halo of sickly, bright radiance. Overlay schematics told Kiran that two of his vessels

closest to the planet had already been overwhelmed and immolated by the outrushing energies ripping from the planetary sphere. He waited, braced, knowing that he was about to see the planet blow apart.

But it did not.

A second planet had appeared beside it instead, smaller, like a conjoined twin, so closely nestled against the larger globe of Ardamantua that it looked like a swollen, cancerous growth extending from the target world.

It was the phantom, the auspex phantom, the so-called imaging artifact.

It was the ghost moon. And it had finally manifested, solid and real.

'I don't understand what I'm seeing,' murmured Lord Commander Militant Heth.

'I do,' said Kiran. Alert overlays, bright red, zoomed in on the display to triangulate and identify hundreds of tiny shapes that rushed from the new moon like missiles.

He didn't need the overlays. He had already seen them.

They were ships. They were warships.

They powered out of the gravity storm of nearspace towards his fleet in attack formation.

'Gunnery! Gunnery!' he bellowed. 'Weapons to bear! Now!'

# TWENTY-EIGHT

## Ardamantua

A blast of stunning sound and pressure swept across the stockade.

The force shredded parts of the fabricated structure and spilled over many of the stone blocks and boulders that Algerin's survivors had expertly stacked into protective walls. It was an overpressure burst, the sort of concussion that might have accompanied a multi-megaton detonation on a neighbouring landmass. The wall of the blast travelled through the anguished atmosphere of Ardamantua like a sonic tidal wave, crossing continents, swirling seas, lifting soil, stripping vegetation and levelling forests.

It was accompanied by the longest, loudest noise burst of all, a burst that every living thing on Ardamantua could feel in its guts and in its diaphragm. It shook internal organs, even those encased in the transhumanly reinforced and plate-armoured bodies of the Adeptus Astartes. It made eardrums burst and noses bleed. It burrowed into brains like iron spikes.

In the blisternest chamber, the tech-adept had risen triumphantly to his feet, the jack cables straining at his sockets, his arms outstretched as he howled the words aloud.

'I am Slaughter! *I am Slaughter!*'

The magos biologis' makeshift apparatus was beginning to malfunction. Connections were shorting out and monitor screens were rolling, blanking or dissolving into squares of hissing white noise.

Laurentis and Nyman had fallen, clutching their ears in agony. The ground shook. The walls reverberated and cracked at the huge atmospheric disturbance passing over the stockade. Fragments of the blisternest material, translucent and grey, dropped out of the deforming walls and the curve of the fracturing ceiling. Daylight and Slaughter began to move up the tunnel to the surface to learn the nature of the crisis, but the rushing, concussive force of the wind drove them back.

Then the wind and the noise were gone, abruptly gone, and the vibration began to ease. The tech-adept stopped speaking forever and collapsed, snapping out the last of his plugs with the slack motion of his body.

Daylight and Slaughter rushed to the surface, their steel-cased boots thundering along the xenos-woven flooring.

Threads of vapour hung in a twilight world. The stockade was ruined. The brothers on the surface had been more grievously mauled by the overpressure than those, like Daylight and Slaughter, who had benefited from the comparative shelter of the nest tunnels.

The sky was a sickly, blotchy colour, like bruised flesh. All cloud cover seemed to have disappeared, and the wind had dropped. It was hard to think where all the clouds could have gone to. There was an odd, loud buzzing sound in the air, and a thin, pitiless rain fell straight down, hard and cold.

The moon hung above them, filling the sky. It was vast and black. It seemed so close that it must be resting on the rim of Ardamantua, propped up on the planet's mountain peaks. That was just an illusion, of course, but no heavenly body could ever be so close to another without some form of technical suspension or energetic holding field far beyond the capabilities of Imperial humanity.

Daylight and Slaughter could see the surface of the moon, gnarled and interwoven, a vast pattern of fused wreckage and interconnected metal plates. It looked like a giant clockwork mechanism, half-rusted, or some intricate toy planet whose brightly painted cover had been removed to expose the inner workings.

Daylight saw the ships, tiny by comparison, that flooded out of the moon's interior into the sky. They looked like insects swarming in their masses, coming out of their colony mound on the one hot day of the year to take wing and migrate.

Thousands. There were thousands of them.

They were too far away to identify with any confidence, but Daylight had enough of a grasp of comparative scale to know that some of them were smaller atmospheric aircraft, and some were vast void-capable warships.

They were seeing an attack formation, a multi-strand attack designed to hit surface and nearspace targets simultaneously.

A rapid-deployment raid of huge magnitude.

An attack on a planetary level.

An invasion force.

Daylight heard the whistle of high-altitude munitions auguring in. The first blasts ripped through the hills above the stockade, turning them into steam and light. Monumental cannons, vast missile arrays and planet-slicing beam weapons were being fired at the surface from the invading moon and the fleets of attack ships it was disgorging.

Bombs rained down, chewing their way across the valley in mushrooms of smoke, or hurling water from the lake in towering columns. Stabbing beams of light raked in from high above, vaporising ground targets and scoring deep canyons of blackened, fused glass in the rock.

'Rally! Rally!' Daylight yelled. He couldn't see First Captain Algerin anywhere, but what little force the Imperial Fists had left needed to be focused and directed.

Projectiles smashed into the countryside around them like meteors. They fell like giant bombs, but they didn't detonate on impact. Thunderclap concussions blasted out from each strike.

'Landers! Troop landers!' Slaughter cried.

Daylight didn't argue. The enemy, this brand new enemy, was deploying in unimaginable strength. Daylight saw the first of them appear, flooding from the impact crater of one of their lander projectiles.

Smoke washed the air, but he could see their ground forces distinctly. He could see what kind of creatures they were. The face of the enemy, revealed at last.

It either made no sense, or it made the worst sense

of all. Daylight *knew* this enemy. Every brother of the shield-corps knew this enemy. Warriors of the Adeptus Astartes might almost regard such a foe contemptuously due to over-familiarity.

Except this particular foe never operated in this *particular* manner. It simply didn't. It *couldn't*.

There was no more time for questions. The roaring enemy was upon them, and all that remained was war.

Daylight drew his sword.

'Daylight Wall stands forever,' he voxed. 'No wall stands against it. Bring them down.'

# TWENTY-NINE

## Terra – The Imperial Palace

An individual was more vulnerable when he or she was alone. That was basic.

The Officio taught its agents and operatives to watch the behaviour patterns of a target patiently and methodically, learn their routines, and then carry out the play when the individual was most vulnerable.

Alone. In a bath, perhaps, or a bedchamber. On a retreat to a country property, or in transit in a small craft. When at his ease or relaxing, his guard down. Eating, that was a good moment.

Approaching a target when he or she was accompanied by other people made things much more difficult. The play might be compromised. A definitive killing action might not be possible. The individual might be surrounded by bodyguards, retainers or a security retinue. Whoever they turned out to be, and whatever their level of expertise, vigilance and reaction, they were witnesses. The presence of others increased the agent's vulnerability. It reduced the chances

of success, or anonymity. It reduced the chances of finishing the play and withdrawing alive.

There were eighty-four thousand, two hundred and forty-seven people with Lord High Admiral Lansung when Vangorich approached him. Vangorich knew the figure precisely because he had swept the immense domed chamber with a miniature sensor drone.

He knew exactly what he was doing.

Lansung, dressed in the gold and scarlet robes of the Winter Harvest Battlefleet, had just finished delivering the commencement speech at the Imperial College of Fleet Strategy, and the vast audience of immaculate cadets and staffers was still applauding. Golden cherub servitors flew overhead among the banners and streamers, clashing cymbals and playing fanfares on long silver trumpets. Lansung was coming off-stage with his armsmen around him: twelve bodyguards from the Navy's *Royal Barque* division. The *Royal Barque* was the name of a mythical, or rather conceptual, ship of the fleet. It was not an actual, physical vessel, though it had a serial code, a keel number and a registration mark, as well as its own sombre ensign design. When a man was selected to join the crew of the *Royal Barque*, he was being recruited into the Navy's elite protection squad. Such individuals were all highly trained and experienced killers, who were then further trained and honed, and appointed as bodyguards to the high-ranking admirals and fleet officers.

They were all tall, stone-faced men in black uniforms with red piping and frogging. Each carried a sheathed cutlass and wore a pair of red dress gloves. One of them, the chief protection officer, carried the admiral's fur shako.

The armsmen tensed slightly when they noticed Vangorich approaching through the crowd of cheering cadets, and the beaming tutors and executives hurrying to congratulate the admiral on his perceptive and inspiring remarks.

'Step back,' one of them snarled quietly, hoping to avoid a scene. Lansung was busy shaking hands with the Head of the Bombard School. Vangorich simply smiled at the armsman.

Lansung, alert as ever, saw Vangorich, and saw he was being challenged. He expertly detached himself from the Head of the Bombard School and swept in.

'Really, Romano,' he said to his armsman, 'you must learn not to obstruct a member of the Imperial Senatorum.'

'My apologies, lord,' the bodyguard said to Vangorich. He clearly didn't mean it. He had not recognised the modest and unostentatious man in black when he had approached, and he did not know him any better now.

'Do you often come to hear me talk, Drakan?' Lansung asked.

'Almost never, my lord,' said Vangorich. 'But I must do so more often.'

They started to walk together through the huge chamber into the mobbing crowd, followed by the men from the *Royal Barque* detachment. Trumpeting cherubs and psyber-eagles flocked after them through the air. Lansung smiled and nodded to those he passed, shaking hands with some. He barely looked at Vangorich as they continued their conversation. Vangorich, for his part, paid more attention to the finely painted ceiling fresco visible through the flags and banners high above, great images of battlefleet ships at full motive, gunports open, crushing enemies.

'Why have you come, Drakan?' asked Lansung. 'Surely not to kill me, or you'd have chosen a less public moment.'

'Oh, you don't realise how good I am at my work, my lord,' Vangorich replied.

Lansung shot him a look. He'd made his comment in jest. There hadn't been a sanctioned Senatorum assassination in a very long time.

'My lord, I'm joking,' said Vangorich. 'Rest assured. Indeed, I chose this moment precisely because it *was* public. I'd have hated you to get the wrong idea if I'd shown up suddenly, unannounced, in a more private place. Things can get so complicated. *Messy.* I don't know what it is. People just get jumpy around me. Must be my face.'

'I'm busy, Drakan,' said Lansung, energetically shaking hands with Lord Voros of Deneb.

'Then I'll cut right to it, my lord,' said Vangorich. 'We need to become allies.'

'What?'

'Political allies, my lord.'

'Why?'

Vangorich smiled.

'I know. It sounds insane. We've never been allies before, and I absolutely know why. I'm not important enough to cultivate. And you, my dear lord, *you* are about as important as it gets.'

'Where is this going, Drakan, my good friend?' asked Lansung, trying to glad-hand others.

'Now *there's* an encouraging phrase,' said Vangorich. 'Indeed. "My good friend." I know you don't mean it in any *literal* way, but it shows me you're willing to make a decent show of civility, and put a good face on a public encounter. That does encourage me. So, let me press this. We need to become allies.'

'Explain to me why before I lose patience,' Lansung said, smiling a fake smile at two august fleet commanders.

'You are a very important man, my lord,' Vangorich said. 'One day, perhaps one day soon, you may be the *most* important man of all. The balance of power you hold in the High Twelve is very solid. You, Lord Guilliman, his excellency the Ecclesiarch. You draw the others around you. None can stand against you.'

Vangorich wasn't blind to the fact that he was standing in the middle of a vivid demonstration of Lansung's personal power and influence, the cult of his personality. The Imperial College of Fleet Strategy, the Navy's most elite academy, was on its way to becoming Lansung's private youth movement. Lansung had been a graduate, and he favoured it unstintingly. All the best fleet promotions went to graduates from the College. In return, the cadets showed the Lord High Admiral a form of blind support that bordered on adoration. Many proudly referred to themselves as 'Lansungites', and modelled their tactical theories after Lansung's career actions.

'The trouble is,' said Vangorich, 'though none can stand against you, some might *try*.'

'What do you mean?'

'It would be foolish. Divisive. But there are some parties, my lord, who might try to oppose you even if it was futile. And that could harm the Imperium at this time.'

Lansung looked at Vangorich directly for the first time, and held his gaze for a moment.

'Who are you talking about?' he asked.

'It would be inappropriate to betray a confidence, sir,' Vangorich replied, still smiling. 'The point, sir, the *real* point, is Ardamantua.'

'Ardamantua? Drakan, that's an entirely military issue. Why is a political outsider like you even slightly interested in–'

'We should *all* be interested in it, sir. All of us. Ardamantua is turning into a debacle. An extraordinary military calamity actually, and we don't yet know what the consequences will be. But let's imagine for a moment that they are the worst *possible* consequences.'

Lansung murmured an agreement, turning to shake more hands and mouth more small talk. He was still listening.

'If Ardamantua turns into a disaster, sir, as you may suspect it might, it may well have long term effects on the security of the Terran Core.'

'We can deal with anything–'

'Sir, the problem as I perceive it... and, of course, I am only a mere *political outsider*... but the problem as I see it is a disagreement *about* how we deal with it. Certain... parties, certain quarters... they see things in different ways. When push comes to shove, they may well disagree with your proposals as to how to handle the matter. They may wish to employ *alternative* policies. They would *fight* you over the correct way to deal with Ardamantua and its fallout.'

Vangorich leaned closer so he could whisper, while Lansung shook hands.

'That might be fatal. Your power bloc in the Twelve is unassailable, but others might be so desperate they would fight it *anyway*. Then what? Stagnation. Impasse. Brutal, political, internecine war amongst the High Lords. *Paralysis*. An inability for the Senatorum to act, to make policy of any sort... just when the Imperium is under threat? In short, my dear lord, my dear *friend*, the fact is if Ardamantua develops into the threat that it really could be, then it is not the right time for the High Lords of Terra to become locked in a pointless, hopeless battle with themselves, with each other. The Imperium must not be left so vulnerable, nor can such a vulnerability even be risked.'

Lansung looked at Vangorich again.

'I may be a political outsider, my lord,' said Vangorich, 'and my seat and Officio may carry very little weight compared to the influence they used to bear. But I will not stand by and see the Imperium under such jeopardy of political paralysis. After all, if my Officio ever had any purpose, it is as the final safeguard against precisely that danger. And that, sir, is one of the two important reasons you need me as an ally.'

The audience around them was clapping more enthusiastically again. Lansung raised his hand to acknowledge them. His armsmen steered him towards the stage steps.

'Oh, they love you,' said Vangorich. 'I'm not surprised. They're stamping and shouting. They want you back on the podium for an encore.'

Lansung turned at the foot of the steps and looked back at Vangorich, who had stopped walking with him.

'We'll talk again, at your convenience,' said Vangorich. 'Soon. Now, go! Go on! Shoo! They want you up there!'

'What is the second reason?' asked Lansung.

'My lord?'

'You said there were two important reasons why I needed you as an ally,' Lansung called out over the rising roar of the crowd. 'What is the second reason?'

'Very simple, my lord,' said Vangorich. 'You may not much want me as an ally. But you definitely do not want me as an enemy.'

# THIRTY

## Ardamantua

Laurentis regained consciousness. He knew at once he was pitifully injured. His neck, throat and chin were wet with the torrents of blood that were leaking from his ears and nose. There was pain in his joints and organs that he was sure would be crippling him into immobility if his nerves weren't so dulled.

He hauled himself to his feet. The tech-adept was dead, and most of Laurentis' apparatus flickered empty with equivalent lifelessness. Major Nyman lay sprawled on the chamber floor nearby, twitching and moaning.

A terrible noise rumbled from above ground. The whole structure shook from repeated detonations and impacts. Laurentis had lived through fearful events in the previous six weeks, and that had included the most appalling climatic upheavals and gravitation storms.

They had been nothing compared to this tumult.

Leaning on the oozing wall of the blisternest tunnel for support, he dragged his way towards the surface to see for himself what new ordeal had been visited upon them. Noise bursts continued to reverberate though the ruined nest. He could hear what seemed like gargantuan warhorns too, warhorns sounding out long, braying, raucous, apocalyptic notes.

The end of the world. The end of this world. It was about time. They had suffered enough.

Laurentis came out onto the surface, into the dank twilight and the rain, and cowered in the mouth of the tunnel. He gazed in wonder at the stockade and the world beyond. The moon filled the sky. The stockade was on fire and overrun. Around him, in the smoke and lashing rain, he could see figures in yellow, Imperial Fists, locked in furious battle, grossly outnumbered.

The place was swarming with orks.

Laurentis had never seen a living one close up. He had only examined preserved specimens brought back from the frontier. He didn't really understand what he was looking at. Where had the orks come from? What part did they play in the disaster overwhelming Ardamantua? Were they another by-product threat that had spilled onto the planet because of the subspace realm, like the Chromes?

Laurentis struggled. He knew he was hurt, and that his mind wasn't clear enough for reasoned consideration. The noises hurt so much. He wished he could make sense of it. Orks? *Orks*?

Slowly but surely, terror began to permeate his numbed body. The intellectual issues ebbed away. For the first time since he had faced down the Chrome warrior-form in the tunnel, he felt true mortal jeopardy.

In life, in the stinking flesh, the orks were colossal. Every single one of them was as big as a Space Marine. They simply radiated weight and power, from the huge knotted masses of their shoulders to their treelike forearms and wrecking-ball fists. Laurentis had never seen creatures express such manifest strength and density by simply existing. They were muscle and power, they were fury and rage, they were raw noise and brute strength. They were truly monsters.

They were armoured in metals and hides, but the armour was nothing like as crude as he had imagined it would be. Hauberks and shoulder guards were expertly woven from steel wire and reinforced animal skin or synthetic fibre fabrics. Seams were precise. The level of ornamentation was marvellous. Shields were studded and curved for impact resilience, and some of them smoked with heat and ozone, revealing they were self-powered with built-in kinetic fields. The weapons, clamped in prodigious fists, were the immense, burnished cleavers and swords of frost giants, not the crude blades of ogres. The huge-calibre firearms were of eccentric design yet superb craftsmanship.

The orks had dyed and painted their green flesh with powders and inks, making intricate tribal designs and motifs. Laurentis wished he could understand what each of the marks and stripes and hand-prints signified. There was something primevally shocking about an ork head dusted in white or pale blue powder, its eyes glistening, its mouth splitting open to expose splintered yellow tusks and rotting molars, its maw shocking pink and covered in spittle. It was an atavistic thing. The ork was the primordial predator that man had fled from when he had lived in caves. It was the beast, the uber-myth behind all other monsters. It was the murderous face of man's oldest, purest terror.

The monsters barked, roared and bellowed as they attacked, their tusked, open jaws as massive as those of grox. They hacked and slammed their blades into the warriors of the shield-corps, ripping Adeptus Astartes ceramite plate asunder. Every blow resounded like a thunderclap, like a slap to the face. The rain sprayed off everything, bouncing off armour, helms and blades, mixing with blood, flooding the ground, splashing underfoot.

Dazed, Laurentis stepped backwards. He trembled. He knew there had been long ages in Imperial history when the greenskin tribes had posed the greatest of all threats to the security, the continued existence, of the Imperium of Mankind. He'd always presumed this was simply a result of their sheer numbers, their ubiquity. He'd never considered the orks to have any potency as a species. They were little more than animals, mindless and unskilled, mobbing in the fringes of the stars, an endless supply of cannon-fodder for Imperial guns in the frontier wars. They were not a genuine threat, not like the malevolent forces of the Archenemy, or the threat of heretical civil war, or even the genius machinations of the eldar. Those were dangers to be taken seriously. The orks were a joke, an annoyance, a bothersome chore. They were an infestation that had to be managed, cut back, and kept down. They were not a critical hazard. They were not... They were not...

They were not *this*.

He understood now. Laurentis understood. He understood

why past eras of mankind had lived in fear of the greenskins for centuries, why the frontier wars had raged forever, why the periodic Waaagh!s had been threats that had caused the entire populations of colonised systems to evacuate and flee, why the prospect of a credible warboss and his horde was something that could make a sector governor or a war-master quake. He understood why, more than any other accomplishment of the Great Crusade, the God-Emperor had been so determined to stop the greenskin threat dead at Ullanor.

He understood why the orks were an eternal menace that could never be ignored.

He just didn't understand how they could be six warp-weeks from the Terran Core.

He looked up. The rain hit his face, washing blood out of his beard. He stared at the manifested moon. Its machined, pock-marked, plated surface was ork technology. He could see that. How? How had they done this?

The moon whirred. Surface features moved and adjusted. Vast armour plating structures re-aligned. Shutters the size of inland seas opened and folded. A huge maw appeared. The stylised image of a vast and monstrous ork face mani-fested on the surface of the rogue moon. Its eyes burned with magmatic light from the moon's core. Its titanic, tusked mouth stretched open wide, and it bellowed at the world below, the loudest and biggest noise burst of all. It was like a pagan god screaming at a sacrificial offering.

*I am Slaughter.*

Laurentis shuddered. He was having difficulty standing up. A hand grabbed at his arm.

It was Nyman.

'What are you doing?' Nyman yelled. 'Get into cover!'

At least one of the rampaging beasts nearby had spotted the magos biologis. It was coming for him through the rain, shield and cleaver raised. Nyman fired several shots at it with his pistol and then began to drag Laurentis back into the tunnels. The ork came after them. As it entered the confines of the blisternest duct, its roaring screams began to echo and resound.

Nyman stopped and fired at it again. The ork advanced. Laurentis could smell it. It seemed to fill the tunnel, head down, shoulders hunched. The rasping tone of its voice was deep, deeper than any human voice.

'Run!' Nyman told the magos biologis. Laurentis tried to obey, but he wasn't very good at it. Nyman had pulled a grenade from his battledress pouch. He primed it and hurled it at the advancing monster.

The blast brought a section of tunnel down, either burying the ork or driving it back. Nyman and Laurentis picked themselves up and struggled back towards the magos's chamber.

'We're finished,' Nyman said. 'Did you see their numbers?'

Laurentis realised he could hear the major quite clearly, because the major had opened the faceplate of his orbital armour.

Laurentis could hear something else, something tinny and thin crackling out of the man's helmet set.

'Your vox is working,' Laurentis said.

'What?'

'Your vox!'

Nyman noticed the noise.

'I... Yes, I suppose it is. The signal's live again.'

Laurentis thought feverishly. He sank to his knees in front of his bank of devices and instruments, and began to reset and adjust them. White-noise screens flickered back into life. He had resolution on several of them, and dataflows Some of them had burned out entirely, but many were functioning better than they had done in weeks.

'There's still gross interference from the noise bursts,' Laurentis said as he worked, 'but the gravitational storm has eased. Yes, look. Look.'

Nyman crouched beside him.

'We've got vox-banding again,' he said. 'And data sequences.'

'Exactly,' said Laurentis. 'All the while the moon was in transition from... from wherever it came from... there were colossal levels of gravitational disruption. The storm itself. The whole of Ardamantua was stricken with it. Most tech was as good as useless.'

The magos biologis glanced at Nyman.

'But now the moon is here, now it is fully manifested, the gravitational flare has subsided. We have a little technology back on our side. Major, can you contact your fleet?'

Nyman had already pulled his helmet's vox-jack out of his armour and was connecting it to the battered vox-caster unit that formed part of Laurentis's equipment stack. He plugged it through to use as a range booster. Static fizzled from the speakers.

'*Azimuth, Azimuth*,' he called. '*Azimuth* taskforce control, this is Nyman. Repeat this is Nyman, surface drop. Do you read me?'

'This is *Azimuth*,' the vox crackled out.

'The command ship,' Nyman told Laurentis.

'*Azimuth*,' he said into the vox, 'We've found survivors from the original undertaking, but none of us are going to live long. There are orks everywhere. Full invasion force. Unimaginable numbers.'

'Reading you, Nyman. Ork threat identified orbitally already. Extraction of your personnel not viable at this time–'

'*Azimuth*? *Azimuth*?'

There was a pause.

'Stand by, surface,' the vox hissed. 'I have the Lord Commander for you, vox to vox.'

A different voice suddenly came over the speakers.

'Nyman? It's Heth. Great Throne, man, you're alive?'

'Just about, sir. It's not looking good.'

'What strengths have you got down there?'

'Virtually nothing, sir. The Imperial Fists are decimated. We're overrun and being murdered. Sir, do not drop or try to reinforce us. You could put every scrap of the ground forces at our disposal planetside and you would still never take this world back. I've never seen greenskins in these numbers.'

'Understood, Nyman,' Heth replied. 'To be brutally honest, a surface assault was not a likely possibility. We're in the middle of a void fight. Assault drop not an option.'

Laurentis pulled at Nyman's arm.

'Let me talk to him,' he said.

Nyman hesitated.

'Sir,' he said into the vox, 'I have the magos biologis from

Chapter Master Mirhen's original undertaking mission here. He wants to speak to you.'

'Put him on, Nyman.'

Nyman threw a switch on the caster and handed Laurentis the handset.

'My lord, my name is Laurentis, magos biologis.'

'I hear you, Laurentis.'

'Sir, if I may be so bold,' said Laurentis, 'you need to do two things. You need, as an absolute priority, to communicate this emergency to Terra. This is just the beginning. Ardamantua is not a high priority target. Whatever mechanism the greenskins have used to bring their attack moon through subspace, Ardamantua is simply a convenient stepping stone, a rest point. Maybe it's a matter of range limit, or power generation. Whatever. They will mass again from here. They will perhaps bring other planetoids through.'

'Throne! How do you know, magos?'

'I don't, sir. I am speculating. But we have to prepare for the worst contingency. Yesterday, we did not know they could do this. Tomorrow, we will learn what *else* they can do, and it will be too late. Sir, you have to transmit a full disclosure warning to Terra. I have some equipment here. I have been trying for weeks to translate the noise bursts. Now we have confirmed the identity of the xenos threat, I can narrow my linguistic programs to include what data we have on record of ork syntax and vocabulary values. Sir, I need to open a direct data-link between your primary codifiers and my resources here. If we work fast, you may be able to include, in your urgent warning to Terra, some actual detail regarding the greenskin intention and operation.'

'How so, magos?' Heth asked.

'By learning, sir, what they are telling us.'

# THIRTY-ONE

## Ardamantua – orbital

Admiral Kiran had drawn his sabre. He'd done it subconsciously, his mind on the fight. The light on the bridge gleamed off its exposed blade. It was a habit of his during a void fight. The sword would play no part in a battle between behemoth warships, but Kiran always felt better with a weapon in his hand.

He had even admitted to his officers, just between them, over dinner in his stateroom, that he had a fear and a shame of dying unarmed.

'When death comes for me, I won't go quietly,' he had said.

The bridge officers manning the stations and consoles around him, diligent and determined, saw the sword come out of its scabbard and knew what it meant.

They were going to deliver death to the best of their considerable ability, but they were awaiting death too.

The bridge of the *Azimuth* was a place of pandemonium. Alarms sounded, most of them notifications of damage to other decks, some of them target or proximity alerts triggered by the attacking warships. The air was rank with smoke from artifice deck fires. Crewmen rushed in all directions, delivering data, or attempting frantic repairs on crashed bridge systems. For now, the strategium was working again. On it, Kiran could see the ships of his line, a curve of green icons hooked like a claw into the nearspace region of Ardamantua. He could see the enemy too, a blizzard of red icons spilling from the hazard marker of the rogue moon.

The taskforce fleet was outnumbered thirty or forty ships to one. A bridge officer did not need years of training at the Imperial College of Fleet Strategy to know how this was going to end.

'The odds are too great,' said Maskar. 'We run. Obviously, we run.'

Kiran shook his head.

'No time, sir. They'd bring us down stone dead before we ever made it to translation.'

'Then what?' asked Maskar, horrified.

'Tell the Lord Commander to make a full statement of the events as we know them, and send it via astropathic link as fast as possible. I will buy him as much time as I can, but it won't be long. We will take as many of them with us as we can, general.'

Maskar looked at him.

'Quickly,' Kiran said, tightening his grip on his sword.

Maskar saluted him. Kiran saluted back. The Astra Militarum commander turned and hurried towards Heth, who was at the vox-station across the bridge.

'Gunnery!' Kiran yelled.

'Gunnery, aye!'

'Status?'

'Status effective!'

'Target selection is now at my station. Primary batteries live.'

'Primary live, aye!'

'Secondary batteries may fire at will.' Kiran drew his free hand across the touch-sensitive hololithic plate of his console, aligning targets in order of priority.

'Autoloaders live!' a sub-commander called out.

'Gunports open!' yelled another.

'Let's kill them,' said Admiral Kiran. He stabbed his finger at the glass to activate the first pre-programmed firing sequence.

The *Azimuth*'s main forward batteries and spinal mount fired. The recoil stresses made the vast ship's superstructure groan. Beams of energy lashed out from the ship, followed by slower-moving shoals of missiles and void torpedoes.

An ork warship died in a ball of light, like a sun going nova. A second ship ripped open, spilling its mechanical guts into the void in a cloud of oil and gas and flame, tumbling end over end, inertial stability lost.

Kiran tapped the second sequence. He was already loading a third, a fourth, a fifth, a sixth, his eyes never leaving the complex mapping of the strategium display. Two more kills. Then another two. The *Azimuth*'s shields began to reach saturation.

He ordered them forwards on their coursing plasma engines. The real space drive swept them in to meet the rising enemy swarm. To port, one of his frigates was engulfed and annihilated. A second later, the fleet tender suffered a shield failure, and was lost in a puff of superhot gas and vapour. To starboard, the grand cruiser *Dubrovnic* fended off swarms of ork boarding ships as it targeted and slew three bulk warships with its main batteries. It took the third with a passing broadside that shredded the monstrous attacker.

Kiran saw the massive ork cruiser hoving in on an attack vector.

'Focus shield strength!' he yelled. 'Starboard bearing!'

The cruiser began shelling and lacing the void with beam-fire. The *Azimuth* shook, shields flaring, straining.

Maskar crossed the shuddering deck to join Lord Commander Militant Heth.

'Summon the astropaths,' Heth told him without looking up from the communication console. 'We have to make this good. There will be data to send. As much as we can code and packet.'

'Yes, sir,' said Maskar. He signalled to aides to prepare the astropath chamber.

'Look,' said Heth, gesturing to the comms console. 'Look at this.' Various images were displayed on adjacent pict monitors. One was of the rogue moon, showing the macabre ork visage that had been mechanically created to glare out at them. Maskar could hear both coded transmission signals and noise bursts running through the vox-caster station.

'Help from the surface,' Heth explained. 'The magos biologis. We're unravelling some of the ork transmissions. It's all bloodthirsty threat, I think. Nothing of substance. Just declarations of hatred and pronouncements of destruction. And this began about three minutes ago.'

He indicated one image in particular, and then enlarged it onto a console's main overhead screen. The image made Maskar blench. It was a pict feed, streamed through some exotic form of image capture system, that was being broadcast directly to them. It was a transmission for their benefit, for the benefit of any victims the orks came upon.

There was little sense of scale, but Maskar appeared to be looking into the eyes of the most immense ork warboss. The creature was so mature, so vast and bloated, its features were distorted. Broken tusks like tree trunks jutted from the cliff edge of its lower jaw. It was staring right out of the screen with tiny, gleaming yellow eyes, its jaw moving.

'That bastard thing is aboard the moon,' Heth said. 'It's their leader. I think he's the size of a damn hab-block, Maskar. Saints of Terra, there hasn't been an ork boss that massive since Ullanor. I mean, they just don't develop to that size any more. Look, look. In the foreground? Those are greenskin warriors. They look like children.'

'Save us,' Maskar murmured.

'Too late, my friend,' said Heth. 'Look at the bastard. Look at him. Those noises we can hear? The noise bursts? It's him. His voice. He's talking to us.'

Heth pointed to another display, one that showed the glaring face on the surface of the moon.

'Look. See how the mechanical face moves? It's working in sync with that bastard thing. Look, the lips part and close at the same time. That's amplifying his voice, turning his vocalisation into that infrasonic signal.'

Maskar felt the ship jolt hard as its shields took more hits.

'Oh, hellsteeth!' Heth moaned suddenly. He spotted something new.

Other portals had opened in the surface of the attack moon: three large circles like giant crater rims or the red storm spot on Jupiter. From them, vast, glowing beams of energy were projecting down onto the surface of Ardamantua. Within seconds, they could see something dark and blotchy flowing up the beams into the attack moon.

Heth ramped up the magnification.

It was rock. Planetary matter. The attack moon was aiming immense gravity beams at Ardamantua and harvesting its mass, sucking billions of tonnes of physical matter and mineral content from the crust and mantle.

'What the hell is it doing?' asked Heth.

'I think...,' Maskar began. 'I think it might be refuelling.'

The attack moon clearly didn't require all the material it was swallowing to replenish its mass ratios. Huge chunks of impacted mineral deposits began spitting out of the moon's spaceward surface. The moon was manufacturing meteors and firing them at the Imperial ship positions using immense gravitic railguns. The *Agincourt* was blown in two by a direct strike from a rock projectile half its size. A huge chunk of quartz and iron travelling at six times the speed of sound raked the portside flank of the grand cruiser *Dubrovnic* and ripped away half its active shields.

Heth was lost for words.

'We've... We've beaten them before, sir,' Maskar said. It was all he could find to say.

'What?'

'The greens, sir. We've always beaten them before. Even at Ullanor...'

'The Emperor was with us, then, Maskar,' Heth replied darkly. 'And the damned primarchs. It was a different time, a different age. An age of gods. Damn right we stopped them then. But they've grown strong again, stronger than ever, and we've grown weak. The Emperor's gone, His beloved sons too. But the greenskins... Throne! They've come just six damned weeks shy of Terra. No warning! No damned warning at all! They've never been this close! They've got technological adaptations we've never seen before, not even on bloody Ullanor.... gravitation manipulation! Subspace tunnelling! Gross teleportation... whole *planetary bodies*, man! And they've all but exterminated one of the most able Chapters of Space Marines in one strike!'

'The Emperor protects,' Maskar said.

'He used to,' said Heth. 'But we're the only ones here today.'

# THIRTY-TWO

## Ardamantua

There would be no glory. Daylight knew that now. He had
been foolish to expect it and wrong to crave it. A warrior of
the Adeptus Astartes did not go to war for glory. War was
duty. Only duty.

He had yearned for reinstatement for such a long time.
Like all the wall-brethren, passing their silent and lonely
years of vigil on the Palace walls, embodying the notion
of Imperial Fists resilience, he had secretly and bitterly
mourned the deprivation. He had yearned for so long,
even to the point, on some dark days, when he had almost
wished for a threat to come to Terra, or another civil strife
to ignite, just so he could defend his wall and test his met-
tle again.

When the call had finally and unbelievably come, he had
armoured himself without hesitation and left his station on
Daylight Wall to go to the side of his Chapter.

Making that journey, he hadn't been able to help himself.
He hadn't thought of duty.

He had thought of glory.

Instead, he had found this. A slaughter, a final, miserable slaughter. In the twilight shadow of a nightmare moon-that-should-not-be, in the freezing, pitiless rain, on the blood-soaked soil of a broken, unimportant backwater world, his ancient Chapter was being cut down to the very last man. The venerable order, the illustrious heritage, the bloodline of the Primarch-Progenitor, it was all about to be lost forever. It could never be brought back.

Terra's greatest champions were about to be rendered extinct, and the gates and walls of Eternal Terra were to be left unguarded. The enemy was already inside, terrifyingly close to the core.

Stupidity had led to this. Strategic carelessness, the vain ambitions of High Lords and the complacency of veteran warriors who should have known better and had led to this. A calamity had been mistaken for a minor crisis. An ancient and so frequently dismissed enemy had been woefully, *woefully* underestimated.

What's more, no one would learn from this dire mistake, because no one would live. Terra would burn.

There would be no glory.


The orks were upon them, bestial, roaring faces in the streaming rain. They swarmed across the lakeside in their thousands, raging and howling, blowing their dismal warhorns, slamming their weapons against their shields to beat out the final heartbeats of the last few human lives. Above, low and impossible, the face on the clockwork moon howled threats at the world it was killing.

Rainwater and blood streamed off the visor of Daylight's helm. He tightened his grip on his gladius. His ammo was spent, so he had clamped his combat shield to his left forearm to meet the foe up close and force them to pay a bitter tithe for his lifeblood.

The orks rushed in, tusks bared, spit flying from snarling lips. Daylight met them, drove his sword blade through a head, severed a limb, gutted an armoured torso. Algerin was already gone, a butchered, headless corpse on the blood-black ground. The rain was a curtain, a veil of silver, like fine chainmail. Tranquility was at his left hand, Zarathustra at his right. Together, they formed as much of a wall as they were able, stabbing and hacking, ripping green flesh and brute armour. Zarathustra's war-spear punched through plate and leather, flesh, bone and blood. Broken mail rings and shreds of leather flew up into the rain from the blows of Tranquility's hammer. Blood squirted, jetted.

Daylight put the edge of his gladius through a jaw and a tusk. He back-swung to open a throat, blocked an axe with his shield and stepped in to kill the owner. Too many, now. Too many. Too many to strike at. Too many to fend off. Relentless, unending, like the noise bursts, the gut-shaking roars. Daylight felt the first of the wounds, blades reaching in under his defences, around his shield, from behind. Waistline. Hip. Lower back. Nape of the neck. Upper arm. Thigh. Armour splitting. Warning alarms in his helm. Pain in his limbs. Blood in his mouth. Red lights on his visor display. Teeth clenched, he turned in time to see Tranquility fall, head all but severed by a jagged cleaver, the greenskin whooping its triumph, drenched in Space Marine blood. He heard Zarathustra roar in rage and pain. Daylight staggered. He fought. He swung his sword, even though it was broken.

He said, 'Daylight Wall stands forever. Daylight Wall stands forever. No wall stands against it. Bring them down.'

He said it as though it still meant something. He said it as though there was anyone other than the orks left alive to hear it.

He kept on saying it until the pack of beasts tore him apart.

# THIRTY-THREE

## Ardamantua

Ship deaths lit the sky. Bright fires flared across the face of the attack moon. Some were pale green ovals of expanding light, some messier smudges of flame, drive fuel and torched munitions. A few were massive detonations that spat out expanding hoops of burning gas.

Slaughter hoped that some of them were greenskin ships, slain by the batteries of the reinforcement fleet, but he had a grim suspicion that most were the grave-pyres of valiant, outnumbered Imperial warships.

The stockade was lost. Slaughter had lost sight of Woundmaker when the west wall caved under the ork body crush. Missiles hammered in from the sky.

He swung the ancient sword of Emetris, put it through two charging greenskins, and then headed for the nearest fractured outlets of the ruined blisternest, which jutted like broken drain pipes from the mire. The rain was still heavy. Every surface shone almost phosphorescently with rebounding rain splashes.

Another ork, its face dyed crimson, swung at him. Slaughter ducked the blow, got his sword in, and cut the creature wide open. It fell back into the wet, sheeting water up as it landed.

The Imperial Fist reached the blisternest outlets. He saw a man just inside, lying where he had fallen, cut through the spine and the hip.

'Brother!'

The dying Fist looked up. Severance, of Lotus Gate Wall.

'Slaughter,' he wheezed.

Slaughter tried to lift him, to patch him, but there was far too much damage, far more than even the accelerated biology of a transhuman could repair.

'All gone,' murmured Severance. 'All gone.'

'Stay with me!' Slaughter growled.

Severance shook his head.

'Too late for me,' he said. He unfixed the battered teleport locator from his harness. The power light was still on.

'Take this.'

'It doesn't work,' said Slaughter.

'Not for me. No use to me. But take it. All the while there's hope.'

Slaughter took the locator and clipped it to his belt.

'Thank you for the thought, brother,' he said, 'but I fear we are all past saving.'

Severance didn't reply. Death had taken him.

Slaughter could hear more of the greenskins closing in. He moved on down the tunnel. Two found him there in the alien darkness, and he killed them both with his sword. Then he heard las-shots and a terrible scream.

A human scream.

The chamber used by the magos biologis was awash with blood. Major Nyman was dead, split in half by an ork's sword. Laurentis, stabbed in the gut but not yet dead, had fallen across the precious apparatus, smashing most of it.

The ork warrior turned as Slaughter entered. It swung its sword, but Slaughter parried, deflected, and sliced the greenskin's face off. It pitched forwards, issuing a ghastly, frothing squeal, and Slaughter finished it with a beheading cut.

Laurentis had only a few sucking breaths left in him.

'Finished now,' he whispered. 'The vox just went dead and the link failed. That means the *Azimuth* has gone. The flagship. Lord Heth. All of them.'

'Just us,' said Slaughter.

'Just you, really,' replied the magos biologis. His breathing was very shallow.

'We can still get out, if...'

Laurentis laughed.

'Still trying to make light of it?' he asked weakly. 'We really are in trouble.'

Slaughter nodded.

Laurentis managed a half-smile. Then he closed his eyes and died.

Slaughter rose to his feet and turned, his broadsword in his fist. Orks loomed in the doorway, sniffing and growling... two of them, four, six, more...

'Who's first?' asked Slaughter. 'There's enough for all of you bastards.'

# THIRTY-FOUR

## Terra – the Imperial Palace

'This statement must necessarily be brief,' the recording continued. The pict quality was not sharp. It had been subjected to extreme astrotelepathic transfer and encryption, and there was a lot of distortion. It was just possible to make out the face of Lord Commander Militant Heth. There were other figures around him, though they were indistinct, and behind them, what appeared to be the bridge of a starship. The recording source kept jarring and vibrating.

'The ork "attack moon" that I described has immense capabilities and possibly almost limitless resources. As we have no hope of outrunning the greenskin fleet, Admiral Kiran, whom I commend utterly, has taken this ship in close. We have attempted to damage the so-called attack moon with primary weapons, to no avail. It is both armoured and shielded, possibly by some form of gravitically manipulated field. It is bombarding us with crude but effective rock-mass projectiles. Our scans reveal that the moon is partly hollow, and – internally – not a sphere at all. The attack moon

is simply the physical end in this location of the orks' sub-space tunnel. It is the mouth of a corridor, a conduit through which they can transport potentially unlimited reinforcements and vessels.'

On screen, Heth looked up briefly as the ship he was aboard shook wildly. The pict image blinked off for a second and then restored.

'With the very little time and limited resources available to us, we have attempted a rapid transliteration of the broadcasts being made by the attack moon. Magos Biologis Laurentis, whom I also commend without reservation, has devised some translations which seem reliable. They are all statements issued by the apparent warboss of the ork horde. All recorded transmissions from the ork vessel, along with all of Magos Laurentis's notes and ciphers, are attached to this communication in compressed data form. We have deduced that the orks refer to their subspace tunnel as a *Waaagh! Gate*. That is a reasonably close translation. The warboss refers to himself by a name that is harder to find a single, specific translation for. Depending on nuance, it seems to be "beast" or "slaughter", or "lord that will make great slaughter". I don't think it matters. His intent is obvious and–'

The image blanked again. This time it took longer to return.

'Time's almost gone,' said Heth when he reappeared. He had been cut by something, probably flying glass. He looked straight into the recorder source. 'Study the files I've sent. Study the damned data. For the love of Terra. You need to understand. You need to be ready. The Imperial Fists are gone. They've wiped them out. The entire damned Chapter.

We are finished here and unless you prepare yourselves
you–'

The screen went blank.

'The communique ends there, sir,' said the aide.

Lansung nodded. He sat back and thought for a long
while.

'Send a message directly to Lord Udo. Tell him we require
an emergency sitting of the High Lords immediately.
*Immediately*.'

'Yes, sir. Is that the whole of the Senatorum, my lord?'

'No,' said Lansung. 'Just the High Lords. *Just* the rest of
the Twelve. No others.'

'Study the files I've sent,' the uneven image of Heth was
saying. 'Study the damned data. For the love of Terra. You
need to understand. You need to be ready. The Imperial
Fists are gone. They've wiped them out. The entire damned
Chapter. We are finished here and unless you prepare yourselves you–'

The screen went blank.

'Lights up,' Wienand said. She rose from her seat as the
light levels in her private chamber intensified. She looked
at her silent circle of interrogators. Despite their novitiate
robes, some were far more senior than they appeared.

'That was the latest intercept,' she said. 'It went directly
to the Admiralty via a secure beacon, but we extracted
the data-copy thanks to well-placed friends in the Adeptus Astra Telepathica. Lansung will present it, or redacted
highlights of it at least, to the High Twelve in the next hour.'

She paused.

'I think three things are self evident. One, we must act and act now, without hesitation. The crisis is as bad as anything we feared and predicted. Two, the public must not be informed of the extinction of the Imperial Fists. That is a priority matter of morale. Three, we must raise our game. There is no more time for subtlety. We knew what was coming in more detail than the Navy or any other body. We did not share that knowledge with the High Twelve because we knew that Lansung's power bloc would make it impossible for us to direct the correct and appropriate policy. Traditional and hidebound military dogmas would have hamstrung us and delayed our ability to react. We must determine policy from this point on. We must be the actual and real root of power during this crisis and beyond, or the Imperium will not survive.'

There was silence. One of the hooded figures raised his hand.

'What, mistress, of the rogue elements?' he asked. 'What of them? There are more pieces involved in this game than the main and obvious players.'

'This is a crisis of unparalleled proportions,' replied Wienand, 'not a game. As for the minor pieces, they will be brought to terms, or contained. Or they will be silenced.'

'What, mistress, of the rogue elements?' asked the hooded interrogator sitting at the back of the chamber. 'What of them? There are more pieces involved in this game than the main and obvious players.'

Wienand looked at her questioner carefully.

'This is a crisis of unparalelled proportions,' she replied, 'not a game. As for the minor pieces, they will be brought to terms, or contained. Or they will be silenced.'

Vangorich pressed a key on his data-slate and the screen image of the Inquisitorial Representative's private suite froze, paused.

Vangorich sat back in his chair, put the slate down, and steepled his fingers.

'Beasts arise,' he murmured to himself. 'And as they arise, so must they fall.'

# THIRTY-FIVE

## Terra – Tashkent Hive

It was a snowy night. Out of the steel-cold blackness, bliz-zards drove in and coated the spires of the vast hive as if they were a range of mountain peaks. Lights twinkled in the vertical city, numerous as the stars.

The routines of Adeptus Arbitrator Sector Overseer Esad Wire had been carefully observed for some time. His work at Monitor Station KVF usually ended at around three in the pre-dawn shift, and he would return to his habitation on Spire 33456 via an eating house in the Uchtepa District, which served food after hours.

On this particular day, there were variations. Two hours into his shift, Wire received a personal transmission via encrypted vox, a call that lasted only eight seconds, and which Wire did not contribute to. He merely listened. The nature and content of what he listened to was not possible to ascertain.

Presumably as a result of this transmission, Wire reported to his superintendent that he was ill, the unfortunate flare-up of some chronic condition. He requested, and was

granted, permission to leave work early and visit the district medicae before returning to his hab.

He left the station three hours before the scheduled end of his shift, as soon as the relief overseer arrived to cover him, but he did not travel to the district medicae's office, nor did he travel home. Instead, dressed in his long, brown leather storm coat, and carrying a small but apparently heavy bag, he went west through the Commercia District towards the Mirobod Transit Terminal. The Mirobod Terminal served the Trans-Altai maglev lines.

Approaching the terminal, Wire did not seem to be aware he was under observation or being shadowed. The exterior rail shutters had been opened, and snow was blowing in under the canopy, dusting the concourse.

Wire went down two levels and then, oddly, walked into the seedy basement section of the terminal where derelicts and low-life individuals congregated. Wire vanished briefly into the dank, concrete underlevel of support pillars, garbage and oil drum fires.

Uneasy, Kalthro decided it was necessary to act before Wire began to suspect anything. He left his vantage point, dropped down the east wall of the terminal on a micro-filament cable, and waited for Wire to emerge from the north end colonnade of the underlevel.

When the man in the long brown storm coat reappeared, Kalthro pounced. He brought the man down cleanly, broke his back, and snapped his neck.

The corpse was face down on the filthy rockcrete floor. Kalthro got up and rolled the body over.

'You don't need to pay a poor man to wear a thick coat

on a night like this,' said Esad Wire from behind Wienand's agent.

Kalthro turned. He was very fast indeed. The snub-las was already in his hand. He was, as Wienand had boasted, a superlative operative, the best in the Inquisition's employ.

But, as he turned, he was no longer facing Esad Wire, Sector Overseer, Monitor Station KVF (Arbitrator).

Beast Krule met him with a smile. He touched Kalthro's right forearm and shattered the bones there. The snub-las dropped out of a useless hand. Then Krule put his right fist in Kalthro's face.

It went through. Clean through. The knuckle points fractured out through the back of Kalthro's skull, jetting tissue and blood with them under considerable pressure. The operative's body hung off the fist, twitching. Krule jerked his hand back, and it came out gore-slick and steaming.

Kalthro crumpled onto the floor beside the dead vagrant in the brown coat. More steam rose. Blood pooled, dark and glossy. Then it began to clot and then freeze in the desperate temperatures.

Krule looked down at the body.

'Not bad,' he allowed. He wiped his bloody hand clean on Kalthro's jacket, recovered his coat, and picked up his bag.

Then he walked away into the frozen night towards the maglev terminal entrance, whistling an oddly cheerful refrain.

## ABOUT THE AUTHOR

**Dan Abnett** is the author of the Horus Heresy
novels *The Unremembered Empire*, *Know No Fear*
and *Prospero Burns*, the last two of which were
both *New York Times* bestsellers. He has written
almost fifty novels, including the acclaimed
Gaunt's Ghosts series, and the Eisenhorn and
Ravenor trilogies. He scripted *Macragge's
Honour*, the first Horus Heresy graphic novel, as
well as numerous audio dramas and short stories
set in the Warhammer 40,000 and Warhammer
universes. He lives and works in Maidstone, Kent.

The Beast Arises continues in Book II

# Predator, Prey

## by Rob Sanders

### January 2016

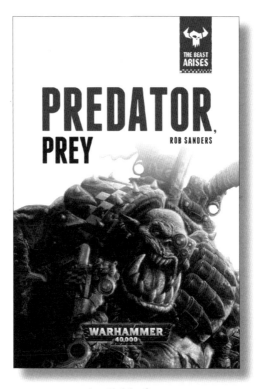

Available from
blacklibrary.com and